A DUKE IN TIME
SAVES NINE

Dukes in Danger
Book 4

Emily E K Murdoch

ARE YOU SIGNED UP FOR DRAGONBLADE'S BLOG?

You'll get the latest news and information on exclusive giveaways, exclusive excerpts, coming releases, sales, free books, cover reveals and more.

Check out our complete list of authors, too!

No spam, no junk. That's a promise!

Sign Up Here

www.dragonbladepublishing.com

Dearest Reader;

Thank you for your support of a small press. At Dragonblade Publishing, we strive to bring you the highest quality Historical Romance from some of the best authors in the business. Without your support, there is no 'us', so we sincerely hope you adore these stories and find some new favorite authors along the way.

Happy Reading!

CEO, Dragonblade Publishing

Additional Dragonblade books by Author Emily E K Murdoch

Dukes in Danger Series
Don't Judge a Duke by His Cover (Book 1)
Strike While the Duke is Hot (Book 2)
The Duke is Mightier than the Sword (Book 3)
A Duke in Time Saves Nine (Book 4)

Twelve Days of Christmas
Twelve Drummers Drumming
Eleven Pipers Piping
Ten Lords a Leaping
Nine Ladies Dancing
Eight Maids a Milking
Seven Swans a Swimming
Six Geese a Laying
Five Gold Rings
Four Calling Birds
Three French Hens
Two Turtle Doves
A Partridge in a Pear Tree

The De Petras Saga
The Misplaced Husband (Book 1)
The Impoverished Dowry (Book 2)
The Contrary Debutante (Book 3)
The Determined Mistress (Book 4)
The Convenient Engagement (Book 5)

The Governess Bureau Series
A Governess of Great Talents (Book 1)
A Governess of Discretion (Book 2)
A Governess of Many Languages (Book 3)

A Governess of Prodigious Skill (Book 4)
A Governess of Unusual Experience (Book 5)
A Governess of Wise Years (Book 6)
A Governess of No Fear (Novella)

Never The Bride Series
Always the Bridesmaid (Book 1)
Always the Chaperone (Book 2)
Always the Courtesan (Book 3)
Always the Best Friend (Book 4)
Always the Wallflower (Book 5)
Always the Bluestocking (Book 6)
Always the Rival (Book 7)
Always the Matchmaker (Book 8)
Always the Widow (Book 9)
Always the Rebel (Book 10)
Always the Mistress (Book 11)
Always the Second Choice (Book 12)
Always the Mistletoe (Novella)
Always the Reverend (Novella)

The Lyon's Den Series
Always the Lyon Tamer

Pirates of Britannia Series
Always the High Seas

De Wolfe Pack: The Series
Whirlwind with a Wolfe

CHAPTER ONE

September 4, 1810

B YRON RENWICK, DUKE of Sedley, groaned as he settled into the comfortable armchair by the fire in his library.

Missed them again.

It was galling. The most provoking part, of course, was he had only missed them because of that fool of a magistrate. If he'd just come when he'd sent the letter—

"A brandy, Your Grace?" asked his butler quietly.

Byron glared, but his expression softened when he saw the nerves on his servant's face. It wasn't his fault the Glasshand Gang hadn't been apprehended—*again*—as they robbed another mail coach. It wasn't his own fault either, but that was beside the point.

His butler hadn't been attempting to chase them down for the last eighteen months.

"Yes," he said heavily. "And a pipe. And something from the kitchen—"

"Cook has already started plating up what should have been tonight's dinner, Your Grace," murmured Wilson.

Byron shot him a look, but there didn't seem to be any insolence in his servant's gaze, so he said nothing.

He had missed dinner. And luncheon, now he came to think of it, Byron remembered as he placed a hand on his growling stomach.

"I would like to ask a question, if I may, Your Grace," said Wilson delicately.

Byron looked up. His butler had been with him ten years—at least, with the family for ten years. There was a certain tone the man had when he was going to obliquely suggest something he knew would be taken ill from any other servant.

With a frown, Byron said, "Yes?"

The butler skillfully cleared his throat as only a butler knew how. "I merely wished to inquire, Your Grace, just how long you will be attempting to apprehend—"

"I will not be attempting for much longer, Wilson; I will be successful!" Byron said with a glare that would have melted the resolve of most gentlemen.

His butler, however, only wilted. "Of course, Your Grace. I will have the brandy, pipe, and plate sent up directly."

And with a snap of the library door, the duke was alone.

Byron sighed heavily, pulling a hand through his messy hair and wishing to goodness he'd had time for a shave that morning. It wasn't his timekeeping that was the trouble. No, it was that judge he'd gone to that morning...

When he'd arrived outside Snee's house, it was in haste. The informant had come by the kitchens at Byron's London residence, so it had taken a full twenty minutes to reach the master of the house.

When it came to the Glasshand Gang, every minute counted.

"I must speak to Snee," Byron snapped, pushing past the footman who had opened the door and looking about the hallway. "In here?"

"His lordship is—"

"I must see him now," was Byron's only response. "Tell the man the Duke of Sedley is waiting and will not wait much longer."

The trouble was, he had. Byron had seethed as he'd paced up and down the magistrate's office, desperately wishing he'd seen the note sooner.

The moment the man stepped into his office, Byron had stuffed the note in his face.

"Have you seen this?"

Blinking in astonishment at Byron's sudden appearance and loud voice, Snee had spluttered, "Wh-What—Your Grace! What an honor to—"

"Yes, yes, we can leave all that," Byron muttered, waving a hand.

That was the trouble with being a duke. One always had to put up with the curtseys and bows and obsequiousness, all the fripperies that society demanded. No one ever actually got to the point.

"Here, read this," he repeated, shoving the note his butler had brought him on a silver platter into the magistrate's hands.

Snee looked carefully at the note. Byron no longer needed to. In the short time it had taken for his barouche to make the journey to the magistrate's rooms across London, he had memorized it.

Glasshand Gang to attack mail coach to Edinburgh tonight.

"My word," murmured the magistrate, eyes wide. "Tonight, you say."

"And we know precisely where they will be, for all London knows where the Edinburgh mail coach sets off from," Byron had said eagerly, chest tightening. "We can finally do it—we can catch them!"

And he had known, in that moment, that the magistrate would do nothing. He wouldn't act swiftly, wouldn't take him seriously, would argue with him for the next hour about the authenticity of the note and whether messenger boys could be trusted.

And all the while, Byron's heart would sink as he saw another chance to catch the Glasshand Gang slip through his fingers.

"Not sure really what I am supposed to do," Snee had finished with a helpless shrug.

Byron had tried, he really had. But it was impossible to keep the irritation entirely from his voice. "You are a magistrate, man. You're a judge; you have a responsibility to—"

"Catch criminals before they have committed a crime?" interrupted the man with a raised eyebrow. "I am not sure whether I can do such a thing, Your Grace."

It had been all Byron could do not to grit his teeth. Trying carefully to keep his voice level, he said, "They have committed so many crimes already! Can you not arrest them on a charge, any charge, from their past?"

"Ah, well, it is complicated, is it not?" said the older man helplessly. "Do I have full evidence? No. Were all the crimes committed in my district? Certainly not. And as for finding people who will testify against them—"

"I will testify against them," Byron snapped.

He was not about to let this chance go. They had to stop the Glasshand Gang; they had to save innocent lives!

"And what better way to catch them than right before they commit a crime?" he had continued eagerly. "Think of the lives we'll save, the damage we'll prevent—"

"This is England, man. I cannot just seize a man for thinking of committing a crime," Snee said a little more harshly. "My jail would be full! No court would allow it! I'd lose my position; my career would be over!"

And Byron had tried to breathe, but it was all so infuriating. "Surely it is better to prevent a crime than simply let it happen!"

"Perhaps," said the magistrate helplessly, sinking into his chair behind his desk and fiddling with a feather quill. "Perhaps…"

And Byron had known, in that moment, he should never have gone to the man in the first place. Snee? He knew him to be essentially good-hearted, but rarely able to think swiftly.

Penshaw, maybe. Perhaps he should have gone to the Duke

of Penshaw instead. He had served the Crown in some sort of capacity, though Byron wasn't sure what. The mere fact it had all been hushed up was proof positive he was a gentleman to be trusted.

Or old Monty, perhaps. Byron had discounted him because he was about to be married, but he was good with a sword. Perhaps Caelfall would have been a safe bet...

But no, Byron had done the right thing and gone to the law. And that, apparently, had been his mistake.

"Really not sure what I am supposed to do about it all..." Snee kept muttering, his gaze fixed on the twirling quill before him. "And really, the Glasshand Gang, very dangerous chaps; might do myself an injury trying to—"

"Forget it," Byron had snapped, finally pushed beyond all patience. "Just forget it, Snee. I'll deal with this."

The magistrate's eyes widened. "You? But you're just a—"

"A duke, yes, I know," Byron had said with a dry laugh. "But I'm no stranger to danger, and if it means taking down the Glasshand Gang, I'll do anything—anything, you hear?"

And with that, he'd marched home, sending the barouche back separately. He stomped all the way home. Home to stew.

Byron's head jerked up as the library door opened and a nervous-looking footman entered.

"What?" he snapped.

It was only then that he noticed the silver tray in the man's hands. Upon it lay a substantial glass full of brandy, a pipe, and what appeared to be that night's entire dinner carefully balanced on a plate.

"Ah," said Byron, covering his rudeness with what he hoped was a broad smile. "Yes. Thank you, ah..."

He stared at the servant, trying to recall the man's name. Well, it was difficult when one was a duke. Servants all over the place.

"Simeon, Your Grace," said the footman helpfully, setting down the tray on the console table beside him.

Byron nodded. "Yes. Good. Excellent."

"And will there be anything else, Your Grace?"

The duke snorted. "Not unless you know of a magistrate who will give me a warrant to…never mind," he added, seeing the look of confusion on the man's face. "That will be all."

It was with a certain relief, from what Byron could see, that Simeon left the room. And, of course, that was to be expected.

Everyone in society had said how strangely the Duke of Sedley—the new Duke of Sedley, that was—had been acting since inheriting his title. Byron had heard the rumors. He'd started a few of them, just for fun, to see how swiftly they spread.

As it turned out, quite rapidly.

But they didn't understand, none of them did. Byron wouldn't expect them to, but it didn't reduce his ire at their callous remarks. If they knew how his own past was inextricably linked to the Glasshand Gang, perhaps they would understand—

Well. There was nothing else for it now. Byron knew better than to just turn up at the turnpike road and attempt to take down the Glasshand Gang singlehandedly. It was too late, the mail coach would be leaving in less than an hour, and how would he find the time to gather together sufficient men?

No, the miscreants would live another day, and rob another coach, he thought bitterly.

Pulling the tray toward him, Byron attempted to forget his troubles by eating the very fine roast pheasant Cook had prepared. Though it was succulent and accompanied by a fine array of vegetables, it was difficult to push aside his troubled thoughts.

It was the perfect opportunity—he knew where the Glasshand Gang was going to be, the very coach they were going to attack! Why, no one would have the same chance to catch them right in the act than—

The door slammed open and Byron, already in a poor temper, glared up at the unfortunate soul who had prevented him from having his first sip of brandy.

"God's teeth, what—"

"Another note, Y-Your Grace, and this time, I had rushed it straight to you," managed Wilson, hand clutching his chest as he wheezed. "A-About the Glasshand Gang!"

Byron rose so swiftly the tray cascaded to the floor, dropping plate, pheasant, vegetables, pipe—thankfully not yet lit—and brandy all onto the carpet. "The Glasshand Gang?"

"Oh, Your Grace!"

"It can all be cleared up later," said Byron with an impatient wave of his hand, heart pounding. "The note!"

Perhaps this was his chance—though it did not make sense. Why would there be another note? What could possibly be happening now?

His fingers trembled as he snatched the note from his aghast butler, and Byron had to force himself to hold it still as he tried to read the scrawl upon it.

Change of plan. Glasshand Gang hitting mail coach to Dover. Tonight.

Dover...tonight...

Byron looked up, his gaze fixed on something not quite in the room.

This was a dramatic change—why? Did the Glasshand Gang suspect their attempt on the mail coach to Edinburgh had been guessed at by the authorities? Had perhaps Snee done something foolish like cancel the Edinburgh mail coach for this evening?

Byron stifled a laugh. He wouldn't put it past him. Perhaps the old dog thought he was doing the right thing, but he knew better.

He'd attempted to hunt the blasted Glasshand Gang for the last eighteen months, after all.

He knew the Glasshand Gang. He knew their habits, their movements, how they would wait until the absolute last moment before they struck. How they were merciless against their enemies and callous to the public.

And he would stop them.

"Prepare the coach."

It was only when Byron heard the words that he realized he had spoken aloud.

His butler stopped gazing forlornly at the mess on the carpet and stared at his master. "The—the coach? At this time—but, Your Grace, it's nearly nine o'clock! It's dark outside; the weather—"

"I said prepare my coach, the one without the livery," snapped Byron, mind whirling. Yes, it was just about possible… "And instruct my valet to gather together two shirts, a pair of breeches, my—"

"Your valet has the evening off, Your Grace," said Wilson in what sounded like the beginnings of panic. "I could ask—"

"You do it then. I don't care what you put in a trunk; just put in something," said Byron excitedly, eyes flashing as he strode across the library.

Wilson winced as a footstep pressed the pheasant more deeply into the carpet. "You are going somewhere then, Your Grace?"

"Going somewhere? Wilson, I'm going to Dover!"

Byron had not intended to sound so dramatic. He really wasn't the dramatic sort—though now that he thought about it, his friends wouldn't agree.

Oh, he knew he was impulsive. Impetuous, that was what his father had called it. He'd never known his mother, she had died when he was very small, but he was certain he had inherited his sense of fun and adventure from her.

But this wasn't mere fun, nor adventure. This was justice, and business, and retribution for what the Glasshand Gang had done to him and his family.

His butler had followed him out into the hall with a worried expression. "How long will you be on our travels, Your Grace? I'll need to know; the number of shirts may be insufficient—are you returning to the country, or—"

"I'm going to Dover, or to wherever the Glasshand Gang is," said Byron slowly.

It was only as he said the words quietly, hearing them echo in the hall, that he realized he really was going to do it.

He was going to catch the Glasshand Gang himself, the law be damned. If Snee wasn't going to help him, no magistrate was. That meant it was up to him.

"D-Dover? The Glasshand Gang?"

Byron ignored his butler and started leaping up the stairs. He'd need a pistol, probably. Gone were the days when criminals like the Glasshand Gang were gentlemen and carried swords— but what was he saying? The Glasshand Gang were never gentlemen, never had been. If they were, they would never have—

"Your Grace!"

Wilson's voice faded as Byron ran down a corridor and threw open the door to his bedchamber.

"Pack," he muttered under his breath, grabbing the smallest trunk he could find and thrusting a handful of shirts into it. "Pack..."

It took him five minutes. At least, it felt like five minutes. Byron's heart was racing so rapidly it was difficult to tell how time was passing. Every throb of his pulse urged him on, because every moment he stayed here, he ran the risk of missing them.

The Dover mail coach. Would they attack it here, in London? On its way? At Dover itself?

Those were questions he would only answer by doing what he should have done to start with. The last eighteen months had been frustration after frustration. When he had been discovered by a magistrate attempting to break into a house he had been certain the Glasshand Gang was hiding in, there had been a rather awkward conversation and then a rather odd agreement.

Serving the Crown was all very well, and he had been rather amused by the vague sort of title they had given him. Investigative duke. It really was ridiculous.

Still, he had accepted it if it meant he could finally bring the Glasshand Gang to justice.

And now he would.

"Is the carriage ready?" Byron asked his helpless butler, still standing in the hallway looking utterly perplexed. "Don't worry about packing a trunk; I've done that."

"But the wedding!"

Byron blinked. "I beg your pardon?"

He may be one of the *ton's* most eligible bachelors, but he wasn't aware he had already made such a commitment…

"The wedding of His Grace, the Duke of Caelfall, and Miss Lockwood," said the butler with wide eyes. "You said you would attend, and it is—"

"Send my regrets—and make them as regretful as you can," said Byron with a twinge of guilt.

Blast, that was most unfortunate. But it couldn't be helped. Though he greatly wished to see that old fool finally brought low by a woman—a marriage Byron himself took a little credit for— this was important. More important than friends, and prior commitments, and weddings. More important than anything.

Wilson stared with wild eyes. "But what are you going to do?"

Byron took a deep breath. "Catch the Glasshand Gang."

It sounded ridiculous when he said it aloud. He half expected the old man to laugh, even though he was the Duke of Sedley and he only the butler.

But his servant merely blinked with worried eyes and finally said in a low voice, "I never thought I would see the day."

And a lump caught in Byron's throat that he had not expected. There was real heart in his butler's voice, and he knew what the man feared. He knew the entire household would fear it once the news had spread in the servants' hall.

Another Sedley, risking their life with the Glasshand Gang.

"I know, Wilson," Byron said, his voice uncharacteristically soft as he placed a hand on the older man's shoulder. "But I'll come back. I promise."

The butler blinked away tears. "I've been told that before."

Byron swallowed. This was getting ridiculous—he was a gentleman, not a milk maid. He wasn't going to cry with his old butler!

Removing his hand from the man's shoulder and clearing his throat loudly, he said stiffly, "I'll try to keep you updated with my movements, Wilson, but it may not be possible until I have successfully apprehended the Glasshand Gang. I am sure it won't be long."

And before his butler had the chance to say anything that may hinder his resolve, Byron opened the door of Sedley Place and stepped out into the night.

It was cold. Far colder than he expected.

Wilson stared in confusion as Byron stepped back into the house. "What the—"

"Forgot my coat," said Byron, his cheeks flaring with heat. "Where is—ah, thank you."

Nodding at his butler who had so kindly placed his greatcoat over his arm, Byron left his home—for the second time.

It was not much warmer inside his carriage. The message to bring around the one without the Sedley arms painted on the side had been heeded, thank goodness, and it did not take long for Byron to bundle his trunk underneath a seat and clamber in.

"Gloucester Coffee House on Piccadilly!" he muttered, tapping the roof of his carriage and settling back.

The carriage lurched forward as his driver urged the horses on, and Byron tried to stay calm and think as they rushed along the London streets.

All he had to do was see them at it. That would be enough for Snee, wouldn't it? The magistrate was right, though it pained Byron to admit it, even in the privacy of his own mind. Arresting a man for thinking of a crime wasn't the sort of thing one did. Perhaps in France. Not in England.

And that meant he had to be close enough to the mail coach to see the crime taking place. Could he secure passage? Bryon wondered. Would that work?

Goodness, the thought of a duke on a mail coach! He almost laughed, heart racing with excitement and trepidation. Now that would be another fine rumor to spread about the *ton*!

It did not take long for his driver to approach Gloucester Coffee House on Piccadilly. Byron leapt from the carriage as it started to slow, almost falling to his knees as he attempted to balance after the change in pace.

Yes, it was just as he had remembered, though with one change. The gas lamps were new; it was strange to see the place so well-lit on this autumnal evening. Byron had read in one of the newspapers that the authorities believed it would reduce the amount of crime occurring on the London streets, but as far as he could see, it only gave the miscreants more opportunities to commit crimes.

It was hard to spot a target, after all, in the dark.

And there it was. The mail coach.

Byron's chest tightened. He mustn't make it too obvious he was so interested, of course. It would be a disaster if he was spotted being so curious about something that happened almost every week.

So despite his desire to rush toward it and shout to the coachman that he was in grave danger—something no one would thank him for, Byron knew—he allowed himself to drift slowly along the street. He looked up at the buildings, wishing to goodness he'd brought his pipe with him. He looked about at those around the mail coach.

And then, before he knew it, before Byron had thought it possible, the coachman suddenly raised his whip. "On!"

"No!" Byron yelled, stepping forward.

It couldn't be. It wasn't yet ten o'clock, and wasn't that when the Edinburgh mail coach always left?

With a sinking heart, he realized his mistake. But this wasn't the Edinburgh mail coach, was it? This was the Dover mail coach, and he had not known what time it would depart.

And now it was too late. The mail coach roared forward, its

famed horses knowing precisely what was expected of them. Fast, and hard, continuous pace through the night.

Byron looked in horror as the mail coach roared down the street and swiftly turned a corner, disappearing out of sight.

He stepped forward without thinking, and—

"Ouch!"

"Have a care, woman!" Byron snapped.

The woman with flaming red hair that he had just walked into glared up at him in a manner no woman ever had done before. "Why don't you look where you're going!"

"Me, look where I am going?" Byron goggled. How could she speak to a duke with such—but of course, she had no idea. He had not introduced himself, nor arrived in the Duke of Sedley's carriage. She had no idea she was berating a duke. "You're the one in my way!"

CHAPTER TWO

ANNE MEAD GLARED. "You are being—"

"Do not say I am being childish, Nancy, or I shall scream," interrupted Beth with a laugh.

Anne had to smile. Her sister's voice trembled, almost stammering over her family pet name, as it always did when she was truly nervous or needing comfort. That was the thing with siblings. You didn't need to say you required their help. You just knew.

Pulling Beth into an embrace, Nancy, as she knew she always would be called by her two younger siblings, tried to put the emotions she couldn't explain into the tight hug.

"You know it's only because I worry about you," she whispered.

Worry about her. Yes, Nancy worried about Beth. She had worried about her from the very moment she had been born, something Nancy could still remember. She had been about five years old—their mother had never been much good at counting—and had stared, in awe, at the screaming baby placed into her arms.

"There you go," their mother had panted, her hair pressed to her forehead by sweat and exertion. "A little sister for you to look after."

At the time, Nancy had been rather unimpressed. Her mother had a year or two before gifted her with a brother to look after, something she had already not enjoyed.

But that was not the point, was it? Nancy had been told to care for her siblings, and so she did. And when their mother had died last year, it had been Nancy to take her younger sister in hand, and to wave off their brother to...

Nancy pushed the thought away just as severely as she pushed the tears away. No. She wasn't going to think about it.

"I still think you are being childish," she said, her voice slightly muffled as she released her sister. "I should be the one to go."

Beth shivered in the dark evening. "And I say you're wrong."

Autumn had been creeping up upon them for a few weeks, but it was only this evening that Nancy really noticed it. The leaves on the trees were golden, starting to fall as the breeze got up. The lamp lighters had done an excellent job, the strange new golden light falling onto her sister's expression, illuminating her resolve.

Nancy's stomach lurched. The resolve she had not managed to make her sister abandon all day.

"We've talked about this," she started again.

"And I have said my piece, and I wish you would listen to it!" snapped her sister, her patience evidently running thin. "You are not the only one who wishes to do something for this family!"

Nancy took a deep breath and forced a smile. Then the smile started to come naturally as other passengers of the mail coach to Dover started to hand the coachman their parcels.

The weekly mail coach. They had discussed it at length, her sister and her. There appeared to be no other safe way to get there, though they had considered then discounted many others.

If only they had not lost the connection with Lady Romeril, Nancy could not help but think. She and their grandmother had apparently been presented to Court in the same year, and the family story was that Lady Romeril had shown an interest in her descendants.

She could well remember their mother discussing whether or not it was right to try to renew the connection with Lady Romeril after their father died.

"She is a lady of great stature in society," Nancy had pointed out. "Her acquaintance may be useful, may help Matthew into university and Beth—"

"But we are in such reduced circumstances now," her mother had said with a heavy sigh. "Would Lady Romeril still wish to know us?"

And so they had not attempted it. It was moments like these that Nancy wished they had. There was no possibility of her doing it now; Lady Romeril likely as not had no memory of her grandmother. That meant there was no one in society to turn to, so she and her sister had concocted this plan themselves.

But that still did not solve the problem standing right before her, shivering in a summer pelisse...

"I just think you haven't thought this through," Nancy said gently, wondering whether calm coercion might prove to be more effective. "After all, you are so young."

"I'm eighteen," said Beth proudly, jutting out her chin. "Almost nineteen."

Nancy's smile really was genuine now.

Ah, eighteen. Well she could remember it. When she had been that age, she had felt as though the whole world lay in the palm of her hand, just ready for her to take. Everything seemed possible. Nothing was too frightening. The world had better watch out, her mother had said. Nancy was coming.

Her smile froze. Well, she wouldn't hear that kind teasing from her mother again, but that was no reason to permit her sister to do something dangerous.

"You may be eighteen, but I am three and twenty," Nancy pointed out. "I am the eldest."

"And the only one with a job," countered her sister, pulling her pelisse tighter around her as the evening continued to chill. "How will the three of us live if you abandon your position?"

Nancy's heart skipped a beat.

Well, her sister had a point. Not that she was about to admit as much to the younger version of their mother who stood before her.

It had been difficult to find something for a woman of her class. They were gentry, or at least, they had been when their parents had lived. Nancy had never realized how precarious one's class was until one lost all means of support.

And women, as she well knew, did not work. At least, ladies didn't.

But she'd had to put aside all hopes of being a lady and take on whatever genteel work she could get.

"I have no concerns of finding another position," she started to say.

Beth snorted. "It took you near four months to find that one! You think it simple to find another household who will permit a lady of letters to—"

"Copying out sheet music is not something only one person in London needs doing," said Nancy severely, pushing aside the truth of what her sister said.

It *had* been difficult to find this position, and it *would* be galling to have to abandon it. But that didn't mean she was about to do the unthinkable and let her little sister go to France!

"I will go," Nancy firmly. "I am the eldest; it is my responsibility to look after you both, not just Matthew."

"And I speak the best French, so it will be far easier for me to go and find him," said Beth with a broad smile. "Ha!"

It was on the tip of her tongue to point out that as it was the English army they would wish to speak with first, it would not matter, but Nancy managed to stop herself.

Beth wanted to go. That was plain, and she had always found it difficult to deny her sister anything.

Besides, there was some truth to her sister's words. If there were...oh, Nancy didn't know, French women who had been bringing food or medicines to English soldiers, then it would be

EMILY E K MURDOCH

useful to be able to question them. Nancy would manage it. She spoke French, just as any lady of their breeding would.

But Beth had always gotten the hang of languages far better than she had. Her sister's French was superior. Her ability to stay out of trouble, however...

"You really have to trust me at some point," said Beth unexpectedly in a soft voice as the coachman called for any last passengers. "I'm not a child, Nancy. Please, trust me."

Nancy swallowed, panic rising in her chest. The idea of letting another Mead sibling go to France, to danger...

But what choice did they have? All their letters had gone unanswered, even the ones to his captain. The last they had heard, he was injured, then missing...

Matthew needed them, and they only had each other. Her sister was right. At some point, she would have to learn to trust her.

"Fine," said Nancy with a heavy sigh, wondering if she would come to regret this. "But wrap up warm, and don't take any unnecessary risks—"

"Other than going to a war-torn country in the hunt of our brother, you mean?" quipped Beth with a grin as she strode toward the mail coach.

"Beth!"

Nancy didn't know what made her do it. It was absolutely impossible to think as the fear of what could happen to both her siblings rushed through her, and that was probably what prompted her to step forward.

She pulled her sister into an embrace that almost knocked the wind from the pair of them.

"Nancy, I need to get on the coach!"

"You just better come back, that's all," Nancy said fiercely, clutching at her sister. "The pair of you."

For just a heartbeat, she really thought her sister would change her mind. Beth clung to her, just as they had each clung to their mother when she had been alive. As though if they let go, the whole world would end, and it would be impossible to be happy again. As though if she just held on tight enough, long enough, then it would be certain that both Beth and Matthew would come safely home to her.

And then Beth released her, and shot her a nervous but determined smile. "I'll bring him back."

Nancy tried to nod, but her body didn't seem to want to obey. "I know you will."

It was with trepidation that she watched her sister be helped into the mail coach by the coachman. This was, after all, the first time Beth was going to be out of her sight for more than a day. They had never been apart. She had never thought they would be.

"Safe journey," Nancy called out, raising a hand to wave as though that would guarantee both of her siblings a safe return. "Be safe, you hear me?"

Perhaps Beth called back to her. It was impossible to tell. More swiftly than Nancy could have imagined, the coachman leapt onto the step and picked up his whip, snapping it loudly into the otherwise quiet London air.

"On!"

Nancy started as the mail coach lurched forward, those who had not been fortunate—or wealthy—enough to purchase a seat inside clinging to the back. The mail coach rattled along the road and was soon out of sight.

Despite that, she stayed precisely where she was. It was hard to believe that it had actually happened. Ignoring all her good sense, she had permitted her sister to do the unthinkable and travel on a mail coach alone!

And that wasn't all—she was going to Dover! Nancy had never left London, and had to assume the provinces had no knowledge of decorum and what was appropriate. And after that...

Nancy's stomach lurched. France. Where the enemy lived, where the war was. Where there were unknown dangers too numerous to count.

Perhaps, if she was able to find someone to take her to Dover, she could stop her sister and—

"Ouch!"

Just as Nancy had turned to look for a suitable person she could persuade to take her to Dover—what had she been thinking, letting Beth go?—a man had walked into her.

But instead of offering her the expected apology, he merely growled. "Have a care, woman!"

Nancy's mouth fell open. *Well! Of all the rude things to say!* He had been the one to walk into her; she had merely been standing still.

"Why don't you look where you're going?" she couldn't help but say.

It was a little bold, to be sure, but then he had been abominably rude. And though he was dressed like a gentleman, the strange look of distraction on his face told her he was not giving her the respect of actually listening to her.

"Me, look where I am going?" the man snapped, evidently furious, though Nancy could not understand why. "You're the one in my way!"

Nancy tried to take a deep breath. This was a mere distraction from the actual reason she had turned around in the first place. She had been wrong to let Beth go, very wrong. How had she allowed herself to be persuaded?

All she could do now was hope she could reach the mail coach in time when it reached Dover. How could she do it?

Nancy's mind whirled. She had never ridden a horse; her parents had lived on what her father called with a wry smile, "reduced circumstances." Perhaps she could pay a messenger? But no, that would never do. Beth hadn't listened to her when Nancy had been standing right before her. What was a letter supposed to do?

"You don't have to be so rude, you know," she said absentmindedly then froze as the man gave her a look.

"I beg your pardon," he said stiffly, evidently not concerned at all about offending her. "But who do you think you are, telling me not to be rude?"

Nancy drew herself up. *Well!* "I am the woman you almost knocked to the ground," she said stiffly. "And who are you?"

It was most bold of her to say such a thing. Nancy knew ladies were supposed to wait to be introduced to anyone, let alone a man—and this man appeared, by the quality of his greatcoat, to be an approximation of a gentleman.

But there wasn't anyone here to introduce them, and besides, she had already collided with him.

The mere thought of that moment brought it back to Nancy's mind, vividly as though it had just occurred. The strength of his chest, the broadness of his shoulders, the sudden masculine scent…

"I am…Byron," the man said hesitantly.

Nancy snorted. She was no fool. "You think to give me a false name to hide your identity? You admit then that you walked into me and did not apologize?"

"What?" the man said wildly.

"You do not have to pretend to be Lord Byron, the poet," said Nancy, raising a finger and pointing it at him.

It was the fear for her sister that was sparking this, she knew, but Nancy felt a rather joyful exuberance at being able to speak her mind in public. Well, ladies so rarely were permitted to do such a thing, were they? And it was not as though she was ever going to see this man again, whatever his name was.

"You know," prompted Nancy, almost raring for an argument, so much adrenaline pumping through her veins after her disagreement with her sister and the subsequent panic. "The poet?"

"Yes, yes, I know Lord Byron," snapped the man. "He's a cousin."

Nancy blinked. *What on earth—a cousin? To Lord Byron?*

Heavens, had she managed to insult one of the upper classes?

There wasn't any chance that she was speaking to a nobleman, was there?

"I beg your pardon?" she breathed.

And just like that, the man seemed to realize what he had said. He frowned, as though it had been her fault he had said something so ridiculous, then shook his head as though dislodging an unpleasant thought.

"Nothing," he said distractedly. "I came here for—"

"You are not going to apologize, are you?" Nancy did not know why she continued to pursue this, but it felt important somehow.

Gentlemen should not be permitted to simply walk about into other people and then not have to apologize. It was outrageous!

The man's dark eyes focused on hers and Nancy's breath caught in her throat. There was a sternness there she had never seen before. A sense of intoxication swept through her.

"You were in my way," the man who had still not given his name said coldly. "I am sorry that you did not notice me."

Nancy's jaw dropped for a second time, but for a completely different reason. *How dare he suggest—*

"But the coach!" the man said wildly to the open air.

Nancy frowned. Was the man a half-wit? The mail coach had evidently departed. Had he only just arrived?

Now that he had drawn her gaze, Nancy looked at the man more closely. He wasn't carrying a parcel, or anything he may have wished to be taken to Dover. Did that mean he had hoped to be a passenger?

"The mail coach?" she said quietly.

The man's gaze darted back to her. "Of course the damned mail coach!"

Nancy flinched. The rude man had spoken with such powerful force, it was impossible not to flinch. But really, the discourtesy! She may no longer be the elegant young lady her parents had hoped she would be, but she was still a woman. It was outrageous that he felt able to speak to her like that!

"The mail coach to Dover?" Nancy said warily.

The man nodded, as though speech was no longer possible.

Although she knew it said nothing of her better nature, Nancy could not help but feel a little relish as she said, "Well I am very sorry, whoever you are, but you have missed it."

The man blinked. "But it can't have gone!"

Really, he was acting most strange, thought Nancy with a prickle of concern. He must not be feeling well. Now that she looked at his face closely, he did look perturbed. And handsome.

Well, not handsome, Nancy thought hastily. It was not her place to find men on the street handsome!

But he was. Oh, in that vague sort of aristocratic way that some men had. A bold brow, a chiseled jaw, hair underneath his top hat that appeared to have never met a comb in its life.

Yet it was more than that. There was a presence to him, something that told her that she was standing before someone important. She had only ever known that with some of the best of her father's acquaintance, although that had been years ago.

Nancy stiffened. *Had her jaw dropped?* Dear lord, she was goggling at a man on the street!

"You do not need to be so horrified," she said stiffly, hoping to goodness the man had been too distracted by the absence of the mail coach to notice her momentary rudeness. "It has gone, yes, but there will be another one next week."

This information, it appeared, did not settle the man's nerves. In fact, it appeared to redouble them.

"But that doesn't matter," he blurted out. "Everyone on that mail coach—they are in terrible danger!"

CHAPTER THREE

"*Y*OU DO NOT *need to be so horrified. It has gone, yes, but there will be another one next week.*"

"*But that doesn't matter! Everyone on that mail coach—they are in terrible danger!*"

Byron hadn't meant to say the actual words. He'd thought them so violently, however, that they appeared to have spilled from his lips.

The moment he had done so, he wished he hadn't. The woman's face fell, turning as pale as the moonlight pouring through the clouds, and her head turned instantly to where the coach had disappeared.

"No," she breathed.

Byron felt that way himself. His insides seemed to be eating themselves up, twisting into knots, painful and full of regret.

He had missed it. After all his fine talk at Snee's, for all his complaints that the man did not act swiftly enough, it had been him who had taken too long to act.

To think, he had just stood here, watching the mail coach! Byron could kick himself. It was most infuriating, and the trouble was, he hadn't expected it. If he'd thought to bring a pocket watch, not leave the house in such a rush, perhaps he would have noticed the time—

Bong!

A heavy chiming sound just to his left. A church clock, striking half past the hour of nine.

Byron frowned. Now, that did not make sense. The mail coaches were always on time, yes, and England was proud of it. But if this was half past the hour, then the Dover mail coach had left ahead of its time. All mail coaches left either on the hour or half past. Always on time. But never early.

Why had the mail coach decided to leave at least five minutes before its time?

"We have to go after it."

Byron blinked. Lost in his thoughts, he had almost forgotten the woman standing before him.

Which was ridiculous. He was hardly a cad—no one in society could call him a rake and get away with it—but he had a fine appreciation for the human form. An appreciation that could be called into question, he would admit, because he had hardly noticed the woman at all.

He did now.

Byron swallowed. Tall, almost as tall as him. Finely-shaped, if that pelisse was anything to go by. A proud and determined mouth, eyes that flashed with decision. Dark red hair that seemed to deepen in color as he looked at it. *Lips that demanded answers,* he thought with a wry smile. *Or demanded something else entirely...*

His reverie was most unfortunately broken when the woman stepped forward with an angry look and snapped her fingers in front of his eyes.

"Hello?" she said, evidently irate, though Byron could not think why. "Anyone at home?"

Byron blinked dazedly. Now that was unlike him, getting lost in a woman's eyes. What was even more unusual was that the woman, in turn, was not equally dazzled.

Could he...heaven forbid, was he losing his touch?

"I beg your pardon?" he said as icily as he could manage.

"You are forgiven," she snapped.

Byron's gaze focused as irritation flickered around his heart.

"I wasn't actually apologizing."

"Oh, what a shame, you were doing so well," said the woman with a ferocity that almost made Byron want to step back.

Where on earth had she come from? And couldn't she see that...

But no, of course. They had not been introduced—at least, Byron had not introduced himself; there was no one else here who could perform such an act.

And that meant...

A slow smile crept across Byron's lips. *Well, this was perfect.* That was the trouble with being an investigative duke. One always seemed to be recognized. Perhaps he could do something about that—stop attending Lady Romeril's card parties, for example. But they were so pleasant. The wine so good. The card players so terrible. The women so pretty.

In fact, Byron had found it altogether impossible to give up almost all his social engagements. It had led, as he had tried to complain to Chantmarle, not once but twice, to being recognized almost everywhere he went.

An occupational hazard for a duke. A damned nuisance for a spy.

"You are not a spy."

He could almost hear old Snee's voice when he had first recruited him into the Crown's service, when he had been caught trying to bring the Glasshand Gang to justice.

Byron hadn't believed him, not a whit. Of course he was a spy! Sneaking about the place, hoping to impress, hoping to overhear snippets of secrets, catch criminals...

As it turned out, the whole thing had been rather dull. Until...until now.

A horrible snapping sound just before his nose forced Byron's attention. The woman looked quite irate now, he couldn't help but notice. And pretty. Marvelously pretty.

"What is your name?" the woman said fiercely. "Jump to it, man, we both want the same thing."

Byron's mouth fell open.

Well, he was accustomed to forward ladies—at least, forward in the *ton* sense. Ladies who fluttered fans, smirked across a ballroom, and made it known, via their father, that they would not be averse to a dance.

But this!

"I-I beg your pardon?" he stammered.

Goodness, if any of his friends could see him now…

The woman frowned. "To catch the mail coach, of course. What did you think I meant?"

Byron swallowed hurriedly. It would not do to admit to that sort of thing, particularly as he was evidently wrong. What a shame.

"My name *is* Byron, believe it or not," he said, attempting a more businesslike manner. Well, if she could speak to him like that, why couldn't he afford her the same pleasure? "Byron Renwick."

And then he fought the instinct to groan, and drop his head in his hands.

What had he been thinking, giving her his real name? Oh, this was a disaster! Perhaps old Snee was right—the magistrate had always said he was a clever man to have at a dinner party, but useless in the field.

After it had been explained to Byron that being "in the field" was not a country matter, but rather more "in the thick of it," he had been quite offended.

He could see the man's point now.

But for some reason, the woman didn't recognize the name of one of the most recent gentlemen to rise to the title of duke.

Her nose wrinkled. "Your name really is Byron?"

Byron sighed. If only his damned cousin hadn't been so notorious, he was certain the name would pass without comment. It was unusual, yes, but it wasn't offensive. At least, until his cousin had published that god-awful poetry.

Now it was just easier to go by Renwick, or after his father had died, Sedley. But he couldn't do that now. Even if he wished to.

Byron shivered as he pulled his greatcoat closer. The night was drawing in, chill growing in the air. "I told you, I really am called Byron. It's a curse more than anything else; you have no idea how often I have to explain it away. You can call me Byron."

"Byron? Your first name?"

He nodded. "Everyone does. And you are?"

For a moment, just a moment, she hesitated, as though revealing her name was akin to revealing royal state secrets. For another moment, just as confusing and inexplicable, Byron held his breath.

Then she nodded. "I suppose that would make things easier. Anne. Anne Mead."

Anne Mead. Well, it was not a very romantic name, even Byron could admit. But it did nothing to detract from her beauty.

Because it was beauty. Even in the dull moonlight, he could see that. He was no fool.

And it wasn't just the way she looked, though that was remarkably fine. No, it was the way she held herself. Poise, his mother would have called it. Downright boldness, Lady Romeril would undoubtedly have considered it.

Whatever it was, it was tantalizing.

"You were late for the mail coach then?" Miss Mead said stiffly. "I suppose you wanted to put a parcel on it, though I cannot see—ah, your carriage. It's in there?"

Byron swallowed. He was unaccustomed to being questioned like this. Typically if questions were to be asked, he was the questioner.

In fact, it had been a few years since anyone had spoken to him like this. Without a care for his rank, his status within society. It was rather thrilling. Intoxicating, in a way, to be considered just another gentleman.

"Yes," he said aloud, hating the lie but knowing there was no other alternative. "Yes, I wanted to put something on the mail coach and—damn."

"But you said they are in danger?"

Miss Mead's voice was tinged with real panic, though Byron could not fathom why. Whatever letter she had entrusted with the mail coach, it would not be harmed by the Glasshand Gang. *Unless it was packed with five pounds notes, of course,* he thought glumly. Though that was unlikely, to look at her.

That was one of the things Snee had praised. His attention to detail.

And he was attending to quite a few details about Miss Mead. She was clearly a lady—there was a clipped note to her tones that told him quite clearly she'd had a governess as a child. He recognized the signs. Her pelisse was of the finest wool, and there was beautiful and complex embroidery around the hem and the hood. So, money…

No, money at one time. Byron's gaze flickered over the pelisse once more. It had been mended, several times, and by a hand not entirely at home with a needle. That was surprising; if Miss Mead had been born into a family with a governess—a family that had fallen onto hard times, perhaps?

"Once you have finished your outrageous inspection of me, you might want to pay attention to our conversation."

The dry voice made Byron jerk his head up. Miss Mead was glaring, an eyebrow raised, and was evidently unhappy with the way he had been gawping.

Byron swallowed. *Well, perhaps his subtly needed some work.* But still. This was a woman who evidently had a vested interest in that mail coach. She could be useful. She could tell him more information.

"Tell me," he said urgently. "What interest do you have on that mail coach?"

Miss Mead examined him for a moment, then said stiffly, "I placed my most precious possession on that mail coach."

Byron nodded. Well, that was simple enough. A ring, a jewel, perhaps a letter of import—that didn't matter. It was the people on that mail coach that mattered.

Oh, if only he hadn't waited at home! If only he had returned from the magistrate's and immediately called for his carriage. He would have been here an hour ago, more than enough time to pay passage and embark on the mail coach, safe in the knowledge he could do something to save those upon it.

And now…

"Why did you say they were in danger?" persisted the un- daunted Miss Mead.

But Byron was thinking. At least he had come with the un- marked carriage. It would have been foolish to be instantly recognized as one of the greatest peers in the realm. That was only going to cause comment, and if there's one thing he wanted, it was to avoid the Glasshand Gang's notice.

Unless…unless he was mistaken. It was possible. He hadn't managed to get close enough to see the details on the side of the mail coach. *Was there any chance…*

"Are you absolutely sure," he said slowly. "Completely sure it was the mail coach to Dover?"

For some reason, Miss Mead rolled her eyes. "You know, I think we would get a lot faster through this conversation if we took turns to ask and answer questions."

Byron stared. Never before had a woman complained of his conversation, much less demanded that they speed things up. It was unheard of! It was…rather disconcerting, actually. Oh, he would never claim to be the most charming man in the entire *ton*, but he had some charm. Didn't he?

"Fine, fine," he said irritably. "What was your question again?"

Miss Mead quite unaccountably sighed. "Is that coach in danger?"

"Yes," said Byron without hesitation. "Are you certain—"

"All the people upon it?" interrupted Miss Mead, her brow furrowed.

Perhaps if Byron had not been so eager in discovering the answers to his own questions, he would not have immediately barreled over her own.

"I thought we were taking turns," he said sternly.

A flicker of enjoyment rushed up his chest as he saw Miss Mead purse her lips together, evidently irritated beyond endurance by him, but just managing to hold her tongue.

Well, if they had not been having this conversation at night, where the gas lamps spluttered and a few unsavory characters meandered past them, throwing them covert looks...

Well, Byron could almost say that he was enjoying himself.

"Fine," snapped Miss Mead. "Yes, I am sure it was the Dover mail coach. I asked the coach man particularly when we—when I first arrived."

We? So, someone had helped her to place whatever valuable item it was she had put upon the coach, Byron thought, tucking away that information for later. A brother? A father?

Despite his better judgment, his gaze meandered to her hands. There was no ring there. Not a husband then.

For a reason Byron decided not to investigate, his stomach turned over at the thought.

No, back to business. Back to the Glasshand Gang. Back to saving that mail coach from absolute destruction.

"Are those people in danger?"

Byron blinked. Miss Mead had taken a step toward him, most unaccountably so, and he saw with surprise that her eyes were a fantastic sort of green that shifted with her emotions. Blue, gray, but always returning to green.

"Don't make me snap my fingers under your nose again," she warned.

Byron cleared his throat. *He was not going to be treated like a school boy!* "Yes, those people are in danger," he said coldly. "Not that it's any concern of yours, Miss. Your item will probably get to Dover safely."

And then be stolen, he thought privately. But she didn't need to know that. What were jewels to the lives of people?

He had to think what to do.

Part of him wished he had taken the time to pick up another gentleman to work with. Penshaw was out of the question, but Chantmarle? It would be so much easier to have another man about the place.

"I want to help," said Miss Mead promptly.

Byron waved a hand. "Yes, yes."

Would Snee be asleep? If he knew the old magistrate, he was probably still awake at this time, drinking in his study and thinking about all his old cases.

"I said, I will help."

"Yes, very admirable," he said distractedly, not taking in a word.

There were other magistrates, of course. Though Snee may not forgive him for the slight, it was tempting to find one a little younger, with a little more grit, who could accompany him.

For Byron knew what he had to do. He had to chase after that mail coach. Whether he managed to catch it or not was entirely a different matter, but just attempting to catch it would settle his conscience.

Then all he would have to do was—

"I said, you idiot, I am going to help you!"

Byron gasped as a woman's hand took his arm. He looked down, saw Miss Mead's fingers there, and tried not to notice the rush of warmth that cascaded from his limb into his fingertips.

She was touching him…

Fine, albeit through his greatcoat, coat, and shirt. But still. Byron had never been accosted so in his life!

"You say those people are in danger? Well, I simply won't let that happen," Miss Mead said fiercely, her eyes unflinching as she looked into his own. "Whatever it takes, sir, I will do. I will not let you down."

Which was all very well, Byron thought wretchedly, but what was a woman supposed to do?

"You can't help me," he started. "You can't fight, for a start—"

And he flinched as Miss Mead tightened her grip on his arm.

"I don't let go of something once I am determined."

Byron fought the urge to pull away. It was strange, this heady mixture of determination and arrogance of the woman. If it were anyone else, he would have laughed. The very idea that a woman could help him!

But as he looked deep into her eyes, he could not deny the ferocity within them. Yes, if any woman could do something as impressive as bring down the Glasshand Gang—

What was he thinking? He wouldn't take a woman into danger!

"Absolutely not," he said firmly.

Miss Mead frowned. "Why not?"

Byron opened his mouth, then closed it again. Well, what was he supposed to say? It was quite evident that a woman should not be put into that sort of danger. Why, for all he knew, there was a chance there was already a woman or two on the mail coach. It would be unusual, but desperate people sometimes took that chance, sending a female relative alone on a mail coach if they had no other choice.

Try as he might, however, Byron could not look away from Miss Mead. She was pretty, or at least, appeared pretty under the moonlight. In any other circumstance, the idea of taking a woman with him for aid would be ridiculous. But what other option did he have?

And then a memory, just a flash, forced its way into his mind. Byron almost doubled up with pain. The agony of that night. He forced it down, never to be experienced again save in these moments of weakness.

Fighting the overpowering nausea, Byron managed to say, "No. Absolutely not."

Pulling away from the delectable Miss Mead and regretting he would be unable to pursue her, Byron strode away and toward his carriage.

"Hey there—we have not finished our conversation!"

"But I have," Byron stated as he opened the door and nodded

up to his driver. "You know the route the mail coach will take?"

His driver hesitated, then nodded. "I don't reckon they'd a-changed it since I last knew it, Your—"

"Sir, will do," interrupted Byron swiftly. If he was going to travel incognito, the first way to give himself away would be to have his driver call him "Your Grace."

Campion nodded. "Well, sir, yes. I know it."

"Excellent."

But just as Byron stepped into the carriage, he was pulled back. A hand had grasped at the scruff of his neck and his collar, and when he staggered back onto the cobbles, it was to see Miss Mead's furious face.

"You have to tell me why those people are in danger," she insisted.

This was madness—they had no time!

Pushed beyond all endurance, Byron did something he had not done in a long time. He told the truth.

"Have you ever heard of the Glasshand Gang?" he snapped.

Miss Mead's cheeks were already pale and he had not thought they could be any paler. As it turned out, Byron was wrong.

"No," she breathed.

He nodded sharply. "They'll attack at Dover, if I am any judge, before the contents of that carriage can be safely boarded onto a ship. So, Miss Mead, if you do not mind—"

"I have to sit facing forward," Miss Mead said most inexplicably. "I am sure you will not mind."

And without a second thought, she stepped into his carriage.

Byron stared. *The cheek!* "I think you have mistaken my carriage for a private hack, madam."

His icy tones did not seem to have any effect. "Come on, you're letting the cold in."

Byron shook his head, as though that would remove all dreams from his eyes—but there she was, Miss Mead, sitting in his carriage. "You can't come with me!"

"We are losing time every second that you stand there like an idiot," retorted Miss Mead, tidying her skirts around her. "Now, either you can accept that you are going to have an extra pair of hands to deal with these criminals, or you can stand there like a fish."

Byron closed his mouth hurriedly.

This woman! She was infuriating, to say the least, and would be placing herself in just as much danger as those already on the mail coach.

But he couldn't deny the veracity of her words. Every moment he stood here, the Dover mail coach grew closer and closer to the jaws of the Glasshand Gang.

He sighed heavily as he clambered into his carriage and glared at the woman seated opposite him. "Would there be any point in attempting to stop you?"

Miss Mead smiled sweetly. "Absolutely not."

CHAPTER FOUR

September 5, 1810

N ANCY'S HEART WAS beating so loudly she hardly knew how she had managed to step into the carriage.

But she had. Now she was in a rattling carriage traveling far faster than any she had ever been in. Sitting opposite a man who had been glowering all night.

At least, that's what Nancy assumed. It was difficult to sleep in a fast moving carriage, particularly when under no illusion that one was unwelcome…but then, she was exhausted.

Sleep, when it had come, had been fragmented.

And then there were the nightmares.

Nancy had known they weren't real. Beth had never looked that tired, that forlorn, that covered in mud. Matthew had not lost an arm.

At least, as far as she knew.

But the knowledge that what she was seeing was nothing more than the panicked imaginings of her mind did not prevent Nancy from crying out in her dream.

"Beth! Matthew!"

And they had reached out to her, and of course they had not been able to reach her. And as she tried desperately to push past the hordes of people on what she imagined were the docks of Dover, it was impossible for Nancy to reach them. Her siblings seemed to move farther away, faster and faster, until she was running and their hands were still outstretched and—

A sudden jolt of the carriage jerked Nancy awake.

Her heart was thundering still. Her fingers were clenched tightly in her lap. Beads of sweat were on her forehead, her fingers damp as she pushed back her hair.

Nancy swallowed. It was just a dream. Just a nightmare. She was not going to let that happen.

The man opposite her, Mr. Renwick, or Byron, or whatever he called himself, was still awake. He was staring out of the window, concern furrowing his brow.

Nancy glanced at the window. Streaks of golden sunlight poured down. It was dawn—or perhaps a little after dawn. How long had she managed to sleep? Three hours? Four?

However many, it wasn't enough.

Drawing herself up and wishing to goodness there was a cushion, Nancy tried to ignore her discomfort. Beth would be in a far less luxurious coach, with far more people in it. That was perhaps the best way to think about it.

Besides, *she* wasn't barreling along the English countryside toward imminent danger…

Nancy swallowed. Her mouth was dry, but she couldn't stop thinking about what Ren—Mr. Renwick had said.

"Everyone on that mail coach—they are in terrible danger!"

She could never have imagined she and her sister would ever get tangled up in something as awful as the Glasshand Gang. The question was, how did Mr. Renwick know about their intended attack?

"Mr. Renwick?" she said quietly.

Nancy had not intended her voice to be so timid, but she was exhausted. Besides, Mr. Renwick may not be the Byron she had initially supposed—thank goodness!—but he evidently had money, if he could keep a carriage like this.

He glanced at her, then returned his gaze to the window. "Yes."

Nancy steeled herself to ask the question she knew she must, even if it would bring her pain. "What sort of danger is my—is the mail coach in? From the Glasshand Gang, I mean. And how do you know? Are you a magistrate? Could you—"

"What happened to our agreement?" Mr. Renwick said quietly.

Nancy blinked. Agreement? She wasn't aware the two of them had entered into an agreement.

His gaze flickered over her; evident interest piqued in his eyes. Nancy flushed.

Well! If he thought her determination to accompany him to save her sister was anything to do with—with that, he could think again!

Not that she had admitted precisely why she had barged into his carriage, Nancy reminded herself. And she wouldn't, not for a while. Not until she had any sort of reason to trust a man who appeared to have information beyond what was expected.

Why, for all she knew, he was a dissolute member of the Glasshand Gang who had been pushed out!

Heart quickening slightly at the thought she could be stuck in a carriage with a reprobate, Nancy managed to speak calmly. "I have no idea what agreement you are referring to. And if you think I would enter into an agreement of *that* sort, I can tell you, you are much mist—"

Was that a smile on Mr. Renwick's face? "I refer merely to our agreement to take in turns asking questions," he said lightly. "I believe you have asked me three."

Nancy flushed. *Oh. Well.* That was different. Though it was hardly a formal agreement, it did at least make sense. *Almost.*

"What danger is that mail coach in?" she asked quietly.

She watched as Mr. Renwick shifted uneasily in his seat. Her heart skipped a beat.

Letting Beth get on that mail coach, alone, had been foolish.

She had been a buffoon to even consider it, let alone permit herself to be talked around by her sister. That girl always had the gift of the gab, but that was hardly going to help her if she was faced with the merciless Glasshand Gang.

Nancy's chest went cold as she tried not to think of the headlines she had read about the Glasshand Gang. They were the most notorious gang in all of London, perhaps all of England. Robberies were their trade, naturally, but she had read several accounts of when the men in the gang had not been given what they wanted.

In that moment, they had no compunction in injuring, sometimes killing those who stood in their way.

Nancy shivered. It was precisely the sort of thing her sister, with her resolute sense of right and wrong, would do. Put herself in danger. Give the Glasshand Gang an excuse to—

"The danger to that mail coach is the danger anyone is in with the Glasshand Gang," Mr. Renwick said, his quiet voice breaking through her thoughts. "Robbery, naturally, and in the event of struggle—"

"Injury," Nancy said softly.

"Likely worse," he replied with a sigh. "I do not say this to worry you, Miss Mead. I am conscious that you are only a woman, and—"

"I am sorry, only a woman?" she said in astonishment.

Only a woman! What on earth did the man mean?

Yet there was no shy embarrassment on Mr. Renwick's face at his faux pas. "Yes, only a woman. You cannot be expected to understand the complexities of—"

"I am sorry, Mr. Renwick, but you are quite mistaken, and in truth, quite rude," said Nancy bluntly. It was the lack of sleep talking, she knew, but she was not going to be spoken to like that! "*Only* a woman? Only half the world's population, only half the workforce, the people managing hearth and home as well as paid employment, most of us!"

For some reason, Mr. Renwick smiled. "And what would you

know of employment?"

Nancy's cheeks flushed with heat. Of course, she was supposed to be a lady—she was a lady, she told herself. Just one down on her luck. For the moment.

Still, it would never do to let the man know she had to work for a living, to support herself and her siblings. A man like this, it was clear by his carriage, had never had to work a day in his life.

Forcing down the envy and trying to remind herself that her father had never worked, Nancy said coldly, "I have eyes, Mr. Renwick. Anyone who lives in London but does not notice the many women working—washerwomen, seamstresses, maids—is blind."

Just for a moment, Mr. Renwick looked disconcerted. "Ah. Yes. Of course."

Aha, Nancy could not help but think gleefully. *I have you there, Mr. Clever Renwick!*

"And what's more, I would argue that merely being a woman should not prevent that person from being an excellent creature, just as suitable for anything as—"

"Could you fight, if you needed to? If needs must, if you needed to kill a man, would you?"

Nancy gasped. Mr. Renwick's questions were sharp but not cruel, the calm in his face belying the panic in her own.

Kill a man? Her?

She had never considered it before. She had never had to. Matthew was always there to protect them on the rare occasions she and Beth had ventured out after dark, and when he had joined the army, her sister and her had merely dropped the habit.

But her, kill a man?

Nancy managed an icy smile. "I believe that is two questions, Mr. Renwick."

And just like that, all of a sudden, the gentleman laughed.

Oh, it was music to her ears. Nancy had never heard such a merry sound, nor seen such a change in a gentleman as he laughed.

Mr. Renwick lit up, all disagreement between them seemingly forgotten, and Nancy was reminded painfully just how handsome her carriage companion was. Why, if they had met under different circumstances—

"You do amuse me, you know, Miss Mead," Mr. Renwick said finally. "Most amusing."

Nancy's jaw tightened. Amusing, was she?

Well, she couldn't afford to be amusing. Not now. Not as her sister approached her doom, all in an attempt to find their brother who might likewise be in a sticky situation.

And it was all her fault. If she had not permitted Matthew to join the army...

But then, how was one supposed to stop a young man from doing what he wanted? He was of age, and he had been determined. His heart was set on the army, and to the army he would go.

Matthew and Beth had always gotten into scrapes, and Nancy had always been the one to fish them out of them. Ever since she could remember. Perhaps it was daft of her to think that would end once they had grown.

Nancy sighed, pulling her pelisse closer. Perhaps that was the one trait all Mead siblings had inherited. Stubborn pig-headedness. It was what had sparked Beth's determination to go after him, and her own determination to go after her sister.

Even considering the circumstances, Nancy allowed herself a smile. All chasing after each other. It was ridiculous!

"You know, we will be passing a town soon," Mr. Renwick said unexpectedly.

Nancy waited for the rest of his speech, but it appeared there was no more coming. "And?"

Unless it is Dover, she wanted to say, *what does it matter?* And they surely could not be there yet...

He sighed, as though his point had been obvious. "I can set you down by the inn. It will be easy enough for you to find—"

"Absolutely not," Nancy said firmly.

Who did this man think he was? She was going to save her sister, wasn't she? Did he think she would simply give up after a most uncomfortable nightly carriage ride?

Nancy shifted, her buttocks aching. Well. It *was* most uncomfortable. But that did not mean she was ready to give up.

Mr. Renwick sighed. "Is there any point in telling you—ordering you to get out?"

He spoke mildly, as though he knew the answer, and Nancy could not help but grin as she said, "Not in the slightest. Aren't there any blankets in this thing?"

As she watched him wince, Nancy realized gentlemen probably did not like to have their luxurious carriages criticized. Even if a woman would have thought to provide some additional comfort.

"I think there might be one or two in the case on the back," he said airily. "I will ask my man to hunt them out when we drop you off."

"I am going nowhere," Nancy said firmly. "I am for Dover, and for saving—for retrieving my valuable item."

She met his gaze steadily for just a moment, then Mr. Renwick rolled his eyes and returned to looking out of the window.

Nancy swallowed, twisting her fingers in her lap. Precisely why she had not told this Mr. Renwick why she was so desperate to catch the mail coach, she did not know. It was hardly a state secret, she thought wryly, that she had a sister. Nor would it put Beth in any greater danger, surely, if Mr. Renwick were to know of her existence.

But what did she know of him?

Her gaze flickered over the man whose carriage she had stepped into without so much as a request.

He was handsome. Wealthy, if the carriage was anything to go by. Knowledgeable, or at least friends with the right sort of people, if he knew the Dover mail coach was a target of the Glasshand Gang.

But that did not explain what he was doing here, why he was

putting himself in danger.

"Well, we'll have to stop sometime," Mr. Renwick said to the window rather than her.

Nancy bristled. Was the man never going to listen to a word she said?

"And why is that?" she said icily.

"Well, at some point, we will need to eat. Rest, gain better rest than whatever you managed to enjoy last night."

Nancy opened her mouth to argue, considered for a moment, and then hated herself for closing her mouth without saying a word.

It was difficult to argue with. Her stomach had been growling for the last hour, though she had attempted to put it out of her mind. That was becoming more difficult with each passing minute.

Nancy stifled a yawn. And sleeping in a bed wouldn't go amiss either.

"Fine, we'll stop," she said aloud, as though she were making a great concession. "Briefly, as short as we can manage. But when we depart again, it will be both of us. Together."

Now why did that sound so strange, so bold on her lips?

She swallowed. Mr. Renwick wasn't even looking at her, so it wasn't as though she had to hold his gaze. But there was something disconcerting about his silence. As though he was supremely comfortable in her presence, despite knowing almost nothing about her.

How did he do it? *Or is this a characteristic of all gentlemen?* Nancy wondered. It was not as though she had much experience with them.

Did all men feel as though they were in charge of every room they were in? Did they ever worry about giving entertaining conversation, or did they just expect everyone around them to do it?

"We'll have to have a longer stop at some point. At a town, or somewhere with—"

Nancy's eyes narrowed. "If I wasn't so certain you wished to catch up with this mail coach and stop the Glasshand Gang, I'd say that you were stalling for time."

The words had slipped from her lips before she could stop them. A dark cloud suddenly rushed across Mr. Renwick's face. He turned, eyes blazing, evidently offended by her words.

"If you think I am in league with the Glasshand Gang, you can think that, but you would be wrong," he snapped, cheeks blotchy red with anger. "I-I hate the Glasshand Gang! I will never rest until I—until they…"

Nancy stared. The man could hardly speak, he was so overcome with emotion. What had happened between him and this criminal group?

The likelihood of him being an ostracized member was disappearing rapidly. She swallowed, discomforted by his evident upset.

"I am sorry," she said quietly. "I just…I do not understand why we would need to stop, that is all."

It took a few moments for Mr. Renwick, breathing heavily as though he had been forced to run a marathon, to calm himself. Then, as his chest ceased heaving and the red blotches on his cheeks started to pale, he spoke quietly, once again to the window.

"I am no expert, but I cannot fail to notice that you, Miss Mead, are without luggage."

Nancy blinked. Without luggage? What was that supposed to mean?

He sighed into the silence. "I am pointing out, Miss Mead, that you are without a change of clothes. As I said, I am no expert, but my common sense tells me that most ladies will need to change some of their…their undergarments from time to time."

Now it was Nancy's turn to flush. That he could speak of undergarments to her!

The trouble was, he was right. She had brought nothing save

her reticule, and that only contained a few pounds. She had also, Nancy realized with a rush of regret, left no message with their landlady, Mrs. McCall, nor a note for her employer.

Well, Beth's fear came true after all, she thought dully. She had lost her place. She could not imagine anyone would happily wait for her to just reappear, whenever that would be. She would have to consider how to—

"Miss Mead?"

Nancy blinked. Thinking of her lost employment, she had almost forgotten where she was. The carriage jolted as they turned a corner, still at great speed.

"I suppose I can buy what I need on the road," she said aloud.

Her lungs constricted, just for a moment, as she thought about the additional expense. Well, perhaps it wasn't the end of the world. Her clothes were in a dreadful state, and needed repair. Perhaps it was time she replaced them.

"You look worried."

Nancy looked up. Mr. Renwick was examining her closely, forehead puckered into a frown, as though she were an exhibit.

She tried to smile, but her fear for Matthew, and now Beth, combined to such an extent, it was difficult to ignore it completely. "I am concerned for my...my valuable item, of course."

Beth. Matthew. The most valuable things she had in the world. How would she ever live with herself if she were to lose both in the same year?

Mr. Renwick nodded slowly. "Your...valuable item."

Nancy held his gaze. *Did he guess?* He certainly suspected, though he was apparently far too much of a gentleman not to take her at her word.

He sighed heavily. "Well, we shall just have to hope that we catch up with this mail coach before it reaches Dover."

Nancy took in a deep breath and tried to hold onto hope. "Not hope. We must."

CHAPTER FIVE

BYRON SMILED HAPPILY. It was magnificently luxurious here in his great bed in the ducal bedchamber. He remembered picking out the color of the embroidered coverlet himself. A nice royal blue that shimmered slightly in the—but that didn't explain why his back hurt so much. Or why he was curled up in this infernal position. He could never recall his bed causing this much pain in his—

The carriage jolted and Byron opened his eyes.

Of course. He was not in the grand ducal bedchamber. He was not even at home.

He was scrunched up into one corner of his carriage still jolting along a road, sunlight swiftly fading as the afternoon disappeared. And he was not alone.

Miss Mead was glaring, though her gaze swiftly disappeared off into the distance once she realized he was awake. Soft pink tinges appeared on the apples of her cheeks, the color growing to match her hair, and her chest appeared to flutter.

Byron allowed himself a small smirk. Well, it was a relief to see he still had some impact on the ladies. Even those who barged themselves into his carriage most mysteriously and demanded to be taken with him on a dangerous adventure which they simply could not understand…

"We'll be there soon," he said aloud.

Just as he had hoped, Miss Mead's gaze flickered back to him. "There?"

Byron hesitated before replying—partly because he did not want to lose her attention so swiftly, but also because he was not entirely sure.

His driver, Campion, had been certain he knew the route the mail coach would take. That was all to the good, for it had changed recently. Byron had little clue of its new route save that it was going to Dover and would have to stop at least twice overnight. Perhaps thrice.

Still, it wouldn't do to look as though he had no idea what was going on. That was part of being a duke: you had to be the cleverest person in the room.

Or the carriage.

"They'll need to stay overnight," he said. "The mail coach."

For some reason, Miss Mead frowned. "Why?"

Byron blinked. "What do you mean why?"

It was unaccountable. No woman had ever spoken so boldly to him before; few men either, now he came to think about it. Anyone who was gifted with the presence of the Duke of Sedley usually simpered and sighed, waited for him to speak, then nodded.

It was one of the reasons he had found this sort of work so refreshing. So different.

"Well, my understanding was that a mail coach did not have to worry about rest," Miss Mead said in clipped tones, her eye bold as she examined him. "You know, changing drivers and horses at inns, that sort of thing. Ensuring the post gets there on time. Is that not the point?"

Byron opened his mouth, considered for a moment, and then closed it again.

Blast. He hadn't thought of that. Why hadn't he thought of that?

Because, said a little voice right at the back of his mind that he

EMILY E K MURDOCH

had never heard before, *you have been distracted.*

Distracted? Byron thought hurriedly. Distracted by what? *I am absolutely determined to catch up with the Glasshand Gang, come what may. After what they did to my family...*

And that's all very well, replied the little irritating voice. *But you are distracted, aren't you? By her.*

Byron looked from his hands to the woman in his carriage. A woman, in his carriage—a woman he knew almost nothing about, and yet had made herself perfectly at home. As though there was nothing she desired more than to catch up with the mail coach.

Whatever she had on there must be very valuable indeed.

"I—"

"You had not thought of that, had you?" Miss Mead said succinctly.

Byron immediately bristled. *How dare she!* "It was not like—"

"You came prepared, though. I saw the trunk on the back of the carriage," said Miss Mead, eyes glittering. "You knew you would be pursuing the mail coach, and yet you do not have any sort of idea how they work. Who are you, Mr. Renwick?"

Byron swallowed. "Merely a businessman who—"

"I don't think so," mused Miss Mead, not permitting him to even think about finishing his sentence.

Heat rushed through Byron's chest. She didn't think so? Who was she to have ideas about one above her station?

Too late, he remembered he had been rather circumspect about his true name and nature. Well, it wouldn't do to have the poor miss fainting with delight that she had found herself stuck in a carriage with a duke, would it? And it would only cause chaos if he were to reveal now. No, better to keep that particular aspect of himself a secret.

"I need to get to that mail coach and stop the Glasshand Gang," he said woodenly, wishing to goodness Miss Mead was not so beautiful. It would be much easier to concentrate if she were not. "That's all that is important. And you wish to retrieve a precious item yourself, don't you?"

Now why did he have the feeling Miss Mead was still keeping something back?

"Y-Yes," she said, just a hint of hesitation in her voice. "Yes, something very precious."

Byron extended his arms. "There you go then. We share the same goal."

His gaze flickered over her. Such a shame she was a gentlewoman. Oh, he didn't need to know anything about her, not really, to see she had been adequately born. There was something in the way she held herself, the intonation of her voice, the worn yet costly fabric of her clothes.

If she had been just a woman, he could perhaps have had fun. Passed away the time more pleasantly…

Miss Mead was glaring. "What are you thinking?"

"Nothing," Byron said immediately, the lie causing heat to rush through his chest.

Really, it was most unaccountable! How did she do that to him—make him feel as though his very thoughts were visible across his face?

Their discussion may have continued if not for a sudden change in the carriage. Byron put out a hand as it started to slow and Miss Mead lurched forward, the sudden change almost throwing her into his lap.

Byron tried not to think about how very delightful that would be, and instead knocked on the roof of the carriage.

What was Campion playing at? They needed to go faster, not slower!

"What the devil is going on out there?" he called.

Miss Mead leaned to the side as Campion opened up the hatch into the carriage.

"Sorry, Your—sir," he amended hastily.

It was all Byron could do not to roll his eyes. Honestly, had the man no brains? If his carriage guest had her wits about her, she may have immediately guessed at his true identity!

EMILY E K MURDOCH

But it did not appear Miss Mead cared much about him; more's the pity. "What is happening?" she asked the driver urgently. "Why are we slowing down?"

"Storm," was the single syllable the driver uttered.

Byron hissed a curse under his breath. "Bad enough to—"

"Every coach and carriage from here to the sea will be stopping for the night," said Campion firmly. Byron saw no point in arguing with him—his driver didn't instruct him on being a duke. "The mail coach will have stopped at an inn further along the road—"

"Well then, we must continue!" said Miss Mead fiercely, eyes bright in the growing gloom of the afternoon. "If we can catch up with them—"

"We'll be dead first," said Campion flatly. "Storm is a-coming, Miss, and the horses will bolt and drag us all along if we force them into it. No, best to stay at an inn ourselves. There's one in two miles I'd recommend."

His gaze met Byron's, who bit his lip.

Well, damn the weather! It was too bad their hunt for the mail coach to warn them about the Glasshand Gang was all for nothing—at least, for today.

But if Campion was right, and he saw no reason to doubt the man, the mail coach would be just as stationary as they were. If they were smart about it, perhaps they could use the slight interruption to their advantage.

Yes, Byron thought, a slow smile creeping across his face. If they stopped early, at this inn just two miles away, they would be well-rested. Better rested, perhaps, than the mail coach. They could leave earlier, gain on them in the morning.

"I think…" he began.

"Pull into the inn and secure two rooms for us," Miss Mead stated to his driver. "We'll rest now, gain our strength, and then leave early in the morning. That will—"

"Excuse me," said Byron coldly. "I believe this is my carriage, not yours."

50

He had expected her to be cowed by his words. His tone, certainly, had been icy.

Yet Miss Mead appeared to have no concerns over his dark manner. "You have a better idea?"

Byron swallowed. He did not, as it happened. Even now he could feel the swaying rush of the growing wind against the carriage. There was to be a storm, and it sounded a bad one. His driver was right. His passenger was right.

It was just so infuriating.

"Fine," he snapped, his bad temper getting the better of him. "We'll stay, then leave early."

Settling back in the carriage, Byron tried to think. Thinking clearly would be a great deal easier, he knew, if he could just put all thoughts of Miss Mead from his mind.

You are not going to have her, he told himself. *The last thing you need on a journey—on an adventure like this is to become distracted. You have to get there in time; you have to save the people on that carriage.*

Or witness another tragedy.

Byron's throat knotted as he tried not to think of that awful day. He would never allow that to happen again—not if he could help it.

Before he knew it, the carriage was slowing outside an impressive-looking inn with candlelight flickering through the curtain-drawn windows.

"The inn," said Campion smartly as the carriage stopped and he opened the door. "Miss."

Byron watched, half irritated, half envious, as his driver helped Miss Mead out of the carriage. He had considered jumping out and helping her—but was that just an excuse to hold her hand?

Get a grip, man!

"I had not expected to stay on the road," said Miss Mead primly. "Yet this place appears to be sufficiently respectable."

"I am so glad it meets your approval," said Byron with a grin.

"Come on, let's get these rooms and then settle for the night. We'll be up early in the morn."

Despite her words, Byron was a little apprehensive as he stepped into the inn's hall and was approached by a man who had to be the owner of the place. He had never stayed in a place like this before. Dukes rarely had to. There was always a friend's manor or palatial home somewhere on the road between one's beginning and one's destination. Staying at inns? That was for other people.

And so it was with trepidation that Byron attempted to remember to smile and bow as the man did the same. He wasn't a duke here. Just a gentleman.

"Good evening, sir, madam," said the innkeeper in a deep voice, his beard crinkling as he smiled. "You are indeed fortunate to be arriving at just such a time."

Miss Mead smiled as a maid helped her off with her pelisse. "We are?"

Only then did Byron notice how young she was. Why, for a time, he had assumed she was at least as old as his mother. She had certainly spoken in that sharp, direct way he connected with the older generation.

But now, soft, gentle candlelight fell upon her and as she was divested of her pelisse, he could see Miss Mead was a young miss indeed. Perhaps only twenty.

Something stirred deep within him that Byron knew could not be fulfilled, so he attempted to push it from his mind. This was not the time, nor the place, nor the woman! *Find the Glasshand Gang, bring them to justice...then you can worry about satisfying those particular urges.*

"Oh yes, excellent timing," said the innkeeper brightly. "Our very last room awaits you—and just in time, for here comes the storm!"

Byron stared at the man, words ringing in his ears as the wind whipped up around the inn and the windows quivered.

"Our very last room awaits you..."

"Yes, our rooms are highly sought after and we are fortunate to have the place full almost every night," the innkeeper went on. "And as I said to…"

Byron's gaze moved past the innkeeper and to Miss Mead beside him as the shock of the situation they found themselves in sank into his chest.

Very last room—there was only one room?

He could see by the look of horror on her face that she had noticed the very same thing. Her eyes were wide, cheeks pink, and Miss Mead had brought her hands together, fingers twisting before her.

Oh, hell.

"Ah," Miss Mead said too brightly, interrupting the innkeeper's monologue. "Well, it is very kind of you, sir, but you see—"

"My wife and I would like our dinner sent up to us," said Byron hastily. "We have an early start tomorrow and wish to retire soon."

He did not know what made him do it.

He had barely thought. Byron had not felt the words in his mind before they were already on his tongue, pouring out of him and making the world shimmer on the shock of what he had done.

"Oh, that is easily arranged! My wife will have two trays prepared and sent up…"

And he was not the only one who was shocked. Miss Mead was staring as though he had entirely lost his wits.

Perhaps he had. All Byron knew was that they could not risk being found out as two unmarried people in the inn, and there was nowhere else to go. The storm had arrived; if they were found out and forced to leave, there was only injury or death on the road.

That much was obvious—though it did not appear to be so obvious to his companion.

"My wife and I?" Miss Mead repeated in a shocked whisper.

Byron tried to smile. Dear God, couldn't the woman pretend

for five minutes? "Yes, it's strange saying it out loud—we are just married, sir, and so—"

"Oh, say no more, say no more! I am sure the two of you would much rather retreat upstairs and enjoy your...ahem...company," said the innkeeper with a wink.

Byron almost laughed aloud, but managed to stop himself just in time. Well, this was certainly not what he had expected this evening, but then, there was nothing for it. The lie had been told now—and it was a lie given in the search of justice. He was certain to be forgiven.

But not, it appeared, by Miss Mead.

"Well, husband, lead the way," she said, no warmth in her eyes. "Far be it from me to lead you in our marriage."

Byron tried to smile. "Yes. Right."

There was a single staircase and, after the innkeeper informed them of their room number, the two of them traipsed up in silence. Perhaps, Byron thought wildly, he should have taken her hand in his! At the very least, he should have pulled her hand through his arm.

God, pretending to be married was going to be complicated. He had never even ventured close to the imprisonment before. What did married people do? How did they talk to each other? How—

"And I'm sure you'll want to carry your new bride over the threshold!" came the innkeeper's voice from behind them.

Byron spun around. He had not noticed the man follow them up, but he was smiling so cheerfully there did not appear to be any way to explain—

"Absolutely not," said Miss Mead firmly, grabbing hold of the door handle and stepping into the room.

In the awkward silence that remained in the corridor, Byron tried to smile at their host. "She's very tired, poor thing. Eager to get to sleep—the food, please, as soon as you can."

"Of course, but—"

Byron did not give the innkeeper the opportunity to say another word. Swiftly stepping into the bedchamber himself, he shut the door behind him and leaned against it, breathing out a heavy sigh. Now all he had to worry about was—

"What do you think you are playing at?" hissed Miss Mead mere inches before his eyes.

Byron swallowed. There was something rather alluring about the bristling woman. A sparkle in her eyes, perhaps, the way her whole body seemed to quiver.

"I had no other ideas, and I didn't see you jumping to offer one," he murmured. "And hush. He could still be in the corridor."

Miss Mead opened her mouth, snorted loudly, and then stepped away.

Byron tried to think. The trouble was, his heart was beating so rapidly, thinking seemed the last thing possible. Well, he had made his bed, so to speak. Now he would have to lie in it.

Oh God, he hadn't thought about that…

Looking around the room, Byron saw his worst fears were realized. Though the bedchamber was well-proportioned, though it was elegantly decorated, though the window would undoubtedly give the room plenty of sunshine in the summer and there was a roaring fire in the grate…

"Only one bed!" cried Miss Mead furiously, throwing out a hand to point at the rather decadent-looking bed. "What on earth are we going to do?"

Byron looked at it with unabashed longing. After a night in the carriage and a most uncomfortable nap, the thought of sleeping in a bed—

"I hope you do not think you are going to do what I think you are thinking you can do!"

Byron blinked. "I beg your pardon?"

Miss Mead's cheeks were flushed, her whole presence evidently shaken. "I've heard of men like you, assuming that they can simply give a girl a ride in their carriage and then—"

"It's not like that," said Byron hastily.

Of course, he could see her perspective. It was rather wild of them to be on this journey at all, and the fact that there was only one room available was unfortunate, but none of his doing. It was not his fault. He had hardly planned this.

But he was no rake—no man could call himself a man if he sought to pressure a woman into anything like that. If she knew him, Miss Mead would know that.

If she knew him, Byron could not help but think privately, she may have a different perspective on being bedded by a duke.

"And if you even think about touching me, I will scream so loud—"

"Look," he said desperately. "My name really is Byron, and I wish you would call me that."

Miss Mead's eyebrows rose. "I warned you! I—"

"I am not going to touch you," Byron said with a heavy sigh. "To be quite honest, all I want to touch right now is a bottle of brandy, a hearty meal, and any soft surface where I can sleep. I promise you, Miss Mead—what is your first name?"

For some reason, this question sparked something warm and tingling in his chest, but Byron ignored it. If they could get through this night, they could be back on the road chasing the Glasshand Gang in the morning.

Miss Mead looked at him warily, but evidently considering she was not in much of a position to deny him, said quietly, "Anne. Nancy, to my friends."

"Well, Anne," said Byron, assuming there was no possibility she considered him a friend in this moment. "Anne, I promise you I will not lay a finger on you against your will. I just want to eat and sleep."

She examined him for a moment, and in that moment, Byron wished he could explain it all. The drive within him to find the Glasshand Gang, to bring them to justice. What they did to him, to his family. That he was a duke, and thought her the prettiest woman he had seen in a long time.

And then Anne's shoulders relaxed. "Fine. I'll take the bed. You take the sofa."

"And the Glasshand Gang will take off early," Byron said with a heavy sigh, pulling off his boots and wondering how long it would take for those trays of food to arrive. "So be prepared."

CHAPTER SIX

September 6, 1810

N ANCY KNEW IT was a nightmare.
It couldn't be anything else. The longer she looked around herself, standing on a battlefield in France—or at least, what appeared suspiciously like a battlefield engraving she had seen a few days ago in a newspaper—she knew it could not be real.

It couldn't be.

Nancy would not permit it to be real. Yet the sensation of very real wind seemed to be blowing across her face. There was a sense of danger, of thunder in the air. A battalion of English soldiers in their daring red uniforms were coming over a hill, and—

"Nancy!"

She turned. She knew that voice, perhaps better than her own. It was the voice of someone who desperately needed her, who had put out his arms when a small child and she had always picked him up. Always held him close. Always kept him warm, and fed, and safe.

Until now.

"Nancy!" Matthew cried from what appeared to be miles

away.

But that couldn't be right, Nancy thought desperately as she tried to run toward her brother, her feet stuck in quicksand, mud pulling at her ankles. Because if he was that far away, how could she see him?

And how would she get to him?

"Matthew!" she called out, trying to reach him with every fiber of her being, her bones aching as she tried to pull her feet from the mire. "Matthew, I'm coming—"

"Nancy!"

This time, the voice was coming from the opposite direction and Nancy turned, heart pounding, to see Beth calling her name.

They were so far apart—she could not rescue them both, she thought wildly, trying desperately to think. Matthew, Beth, they both needed her; they were both far away. And she could not reach them.

Panic rising in her chest, Nancy knelt and tried to pull her feet from the mud, but she could not, and her hands were getting sticky and damp and she lost hold and—

And then the dream, or nightmare, or whatever it was, changed. She was no longer stuck in mud, but entangled in sheets. Sheets of silk. They were red, shimmering in candlelight.

Nancy blinked. It did not make sense, and her heart was still racing in her chest. Did her siblings still need her? Was she still asleep? The inn where they had stayed did not offer such luxury as this.

"Nancy?"

She started. She turned in the bed—the dream bed could not be real—and saw a man lying beside her.

"Byron!"

Instinctively, Nancy pulled the covers up to her neck, but it did not seem to matter. She was fully clothed, and Byron had not removed an item of his attire either.

Yet there was a smile on his face, one she had seen before. One which had made warm delightful heat rush through her, a smile that made her feel...seen. She could describe it no other way.

"Byron?" she said uncertainly.

If the battlefield in France was a nightmare, this was still a dream, Nancy reasoned. And little wonder she was dreaming about the gentleman whose carriage she had unceremoniously entered. He was handsome—charming too, in that irritating way handsome men were.

Not that she would ever tell him such a thing, of course. That would be ridiculous.

Not only would it be mortifyingly forward—something Nancy could not countenance—but it would open her up to...

Well. Things she had never shared with a man before. Things that were scandalous to do and just as scandalous to think about.

Even in her dream, Nancy could feel her cheeks reddening. She was lying here, in a bed, with Byron!

No, she wasn't, she tried to reassure herself. This was just a dream. It wasn't real.

Byron smiled. "No, it's not real."

Nancy tried to smile. "You said that almost as though you could read my—"

"Mind," finished the handsome man in her bed. "But it's just a dream, Nancy. You can do whatever you want—whatever you want. With no consequences."

Nancy swallowed. Now this was interesting. Never before had she dreamed so sharply. But perhaps here, in the privacy of her mind, she could say things, do things, she would never have allowed herself to even consider when awake.

And there would be no consequences, would there?

The dream Byron was remarkably handsome. *No more handsome than the real one,* Nancy thought, carefully reaching out a hand and touching his chest. He was warm. How was this dream so real?

"What do you want, Nancy?" murmured the dream Byron. "No consequences, remember?"

Heat was flooding through Nancy's body, heat she had never known before. Oh, it was wonderful to leave all inhibitions behind and know nothing that occurred in this place would ever chase after her!

After all, a woman's reputation was everything. But how could she be blamed for something in a dream?

"Nancy," whispered the dream Byron, pulling her closer. "You have to ask me."

His touch was scalding, yet Nancy wanted to lean into the heat, know the touch of a man without having to risk her honor. And she would be awake soon, in the presence of the real Byron—a man so infuriating she could hardly look at him without scowling.

But this one...

Nancy swallowed, then allowed her desires to flourish. "I want you to kiss me, Byron."

"You want what?" teased the intoxicating dream man.

Fingers shaking, even in the privacy of her dream, Nancy brushed them through Byron's dark hair and felt a frisson of desire rush through her. "Kiss me, Byron. Please."

And he did—and oh, it was beyond anything Nancy could ever have dreamed before. Such warmth, such passion! The pressure on his lips was delightful, neither harsh nor hesitant, and the pleasure that flickered through her body made her moan.

His hands around her, his kiss deepening, Nancy wondered how she would ever wake from such a delightful dream. And it was so real! It was as though the man was actually kissing her.

"I never thought you'd ask," murmured dream Byron as he turned her onto her back, kissing the corner of her mouth.

Nancy reveled in the feeling of the silk sheets—and yet they were rougher than she remembered. She forgot about them for a moment as Byron's tongue teased along her lips, and then she breathed in the scent of him—the very real scent of him.

Nancy opened her eyes. Byron was kissing her—kissing her! The real Byron!

"Byron!" she breathed.

"Nancy," Byron moaned as his lips trailed to her neck.

This was no dream, Nancy thought excitedly, hardly able to take it all in. He was in her bed, in the inn, and they were kissing!

Her hands came together to shove against his chest, pushing Byron to one side of the bed as Nancy hurriedly staggered out of the other.

"What are you—how could you—h-how dare...what did you think you were doing?" Nancy spluttered, legs barely able to hold her weight as she stared in astonishment at the man.

The strange thing was, Byron looked just as flustered and confused as she felt. Nancy tried not to notice the intensely attractive way his hair was mussed about over his eyes, the way those eyes looked hungrily at her, his dark brows furrowed in confusion.

"What do you mean, what did I think I was doing?" Byron said, sitting up. "I would have thought that was rather obvious!"

"You promised me you would not—you have taken advantage of me!" Nancy said heatedly. "As I knew you would!"

How could she have been so foolish? She should have known there was no man she could truly trust. She should never have gotten into his carriage—

And yet, if she had not, would she be this close to Beth?

"I said I wouldn't touch you unless you asked," said Byron flatly.

Nancy pointed an accusatory finger. "Aha!"

"And you—Nancy, you—"

"Only my friends and family call me that," she cut across him, fury billowing in her chest.

Hearing that nickname on his lips? It was not to be borne. This Byron was not a man she could trust. She should have known that from the moment she heard his name! No Byron was trustworthy.

"Fine, Anne," said Byron, just a flicker of anger in his voice.

Nancy tried not to notice how alluring that made him. Why

was it that such an irresponsible man could simultaneously be so irresistible?

"Is this a habit of yours, Mr. Renwick?" she asked, putting as much scathing disdain into her words as she could manage. "Is this a trick you have performed often?"

The man blinked as though dazed, but Nancy would not credit him with having actual feelings on this matter. He took advantage of her! Oh, if Matthew was here—or if their father lived.

But she had neither of them. No one to protect her, no one to fight for her honor, no one to ensure that they could be married...

Nancy's stomach lurched. *Married?*

Of course. That was what would happen should a woman be discovered in a compromising position with a gentleman. *If you could call him a gentleman,* she thought bitterly. It would all be arranged swiftly, with no one any the wiser that the arranged marriage was only arranged because of the fear of scandal.

But Byron would not marry her, she was certain.

Not that she wanted him to, Nancy told herself hastily. Obviously. She had no wish to be shackled for the rest of her life to a man who believed it perfectly acceptable to just kiss unsuspecting women!

"A habit of mine?" Byron repeated, still looking confused. "You think I frequently allow women to force their way into my own carriage, then kiss them?"

Nancy hesitated. It did sound a little far-fetched. "Perhaps you—whatever it is you are doing, it is reprehensible!"

"I have done anything—"

"You kissed me!" Nancy tried to take a steadying breath, but all that seemed to do was emphasize just how dizzy she was. It had been a remarkably good kiss, she had to admit. Not that she had much to compare it to, but still. First kisses were not supposed to turn your stomach and make your heart flutter and your hands ache for him...were they?

Nancy tried to get a hold of herself. It was not going to be repeated—and she was going to make sure he did not forget it!

"I am not even sure that this adventure, or mission, or whatever you want to call it is real," she said icily. "Do you even want to catch up with the mail coach?"

And then thunder clouded Byron's expression. "You dare ask—"

"You dared to kiss me!" Nancy said, hoping to goodness her cheeks weren't as red as they felt. "If you can dare that—"

"The Glasshand Gang are—I have vowed that I—this is no pretend adventure; this is real danger, Miss Mead, and you would do well to remember that!" Byron exploded. "I vowed to catch the Glasshand Gang, that I would bring them to…after what they did…"

His voice trailed away, his fury seeming to censor his tongue.

Nancy stared. It was more detail than he had ever given. The desire for revenge dripped from every word.

What had the Glasshand Gang done to him?

"You…you really are seeking the mail coach then," she said aloud. All that certainty was slipping away as she looked at him. "But you kissed me—"

"You asked me, Anne, not once but twice," Byron said quietly. "I did nothing that you did not ask, though I wonder now whether you truly…I should have ascertained…oh, hang it all."

His head fell in genuine dejection.

Nancy stared. What on earth was he talking about? She would never do anything so brazen as…

And then she swallowed. Oh. The dream. Her dream with the dream Byron…was it possible that she had spoken aloud? That the request she'd made to the Byron she thought was merely imaginary had been heard by the very real man on the sofa lying at the end of her bed?

"I want you to kiss me, Byron."

"You want what?"

"Kiss me, Byron. Please."

"Ah," Nancy said weakly.

Oh, it was the most embarrassing—how had she managed to get herself into this tangle?

And yet it was not hard to understand. The inn's bedchamber was not large, and the sofa was pressed right up against the foot of the bed. If she had muttered something in her sleep, it would make sense that Byron would have wished to ascertain whether she spoke in earnest...

"You want what?"

Nancy groaned, dropping her head into her hands. So he had asked, and she had answered. He had believed that an invitation into her bed, and they had—

Well. Shared fiery kisses the like she could never have imagined before.

This was a disaster!

"I am so sorry."

Nancy blinked. "I beg your pardon?"

"I am sorry," said Byron again, looking up through devastated eyes. "I would never have—if I thought for a moment you were not eagerly consenting, I would never—I am not the sort of man who—"

"I know," said Nancy hastily.

In a way, she was not entirely sure why she did it. It was not as though she wished, particularly, to make the man before her feel better. He was the one who had clambered into her bed! He was the one who had kissed her so thoroughly she was going to feel the pressure of his lips on hers for the rest of the day.

But as she looked at him, Nancy could not deny the genuine penance and discomfort on Byron's face. He had thought himself invited, and had evidently been eager to oblige.

What she should think of that, she was not sure.

But now that she had revealed it was most unconsciously done, the man was distraught. And that, Nancy had to admit, was the sign of a good man.

Oh, fiddlesticks. It was so much easier to hate him if she believed he had no good character.

"I am so ashamed," said Byron heavily, rising from the bed and pulling on his coat, which he had been using as a pillow on the sofa.

A twinge of guilt soared through Nancy's chest. She had not noticed that. She could have offered him a pillow from the bed, but it had not occurred to her. And he had not asked. His manners had prevented him from doing so.

Oh, what a mess.

"What are we going to tell—"

"We do not have to tell anyone," said Nancy firmly.

On that, she was absolutely certain. And as they stood there, on either sides of the bed where so much pleasure had been taken and so much trouble begun, the good sense she had been born with started to seep once more into her mind.

"No one will know," she said, more gently this time. "The innkeeper and his wife believe we are married, and we do not have to disabuse them of that fact. We should be leaving soon anyway."

Byron nodded awkwardly and pulled out his pocket watch. "Yes, five o'clock. We should leave as soon as possible."

Nancy glanced to the curtain-drawn windows. Five o'clock. Another day, and Beth was ahead of them on the road. If she was going to have any hope of catching them, they would need to leave soon.

"How many people were in the mail coach, by the way?"

She turned and saw to her relief that Byron appeared to have put the whole awkward situation behind them. Better to forget it ever happened, that was it. Better to ignore the fact that he had kissed her most ardently, his eagerness for her just as obvious as hers for him...

Nancy told herself firmly not to think about that. Thoughts like that only ended up in trouble. As she could now attest.

"People?" she said vaguely, trying to recall. "Three coachmen, I think, and my—I mean...six, I think."

For a moment, she thought he had caught her mistake. It was a strange decision, now that they had spent the night in a room together, she thought wryly, to keep the presence of her sister on the mail coach a secret.

But there was still something about this man, something he was holding back. Why should she have to trust a man who evidently did not trust her?

"So, nine people in total?" Byron said slowly.

Nancy nodded.

"Well, I just hope we are in time to save all nine," he said with a heavy sigh. "I had better—I'll get Campion up."

And it was only then Nancy realized she had not given a second thought to the poor driver.

"Oh goodness, I had completely forgotten about—where did he sleep last night?"

Well, it was not as though she was in the habit of worrying about servants. Chance would be a fine thing! They had been forced to let their last maid go over two years ago. When one could hardly afford to put food on the table on your own plate, it was difficult to justify feeding a servant.

"Oh, he kipped in the carriage," said Byron nonchalantly.

Nancy frowned. "You seem rather oblivious to his comfort. Is he, what—just one of hundreds of your servants?"

She had intended the words as a jest, but for some reason, even in the darkness of the room lit only by the dying embers of the fire, she could see Byron flush.

Now that was interesting. Was he far richer than he had perhaps led her to believe? Was her jest true? Did he have hundreds of servants? Surely not!

"Something like that," Byron said with a wry smile. "Look, we really should be going. I'll meet you downstairs. I'll pay the innkeeper now. Try not to be too long."

"Byron—"

But he had slipped out of the room before Nancy had a chance to say more.

Slowly, very slowly, she sank onto the edge of the bed. The truth of his words, that they needed to hasten back to the carriage, could not be denied—but she still required a moment alone. After that kiss.

Those kisses, she corrected herself as her heart skipped a beat. And it was all a mistake, naturally, and one that could never be repeated again. Absolutely not.

If only she hadn't enjoyed them so much.

CHAPTER SEVEN

I T WAS ALL Byron could do not to look at Nancy—Anne—as they sat in the rattling carriage.

Mortification still clung to his bones. How could he have been so foolish? Merely hours before, Anne had made it perfectly clear she had absolutely no interest in him. What had been her exact words?

"I've heard of men like you, assuming that they can simply give a girl a ride in their carriage and then—"

And then mere hours later, he had heard her voice…

"I want you to kiss me, Byron."

And he had immediately convinced himself she had changed her mind!

Byron swallowed in an attempt to force the bitterness from his mouth, but it did not work. He had been an absolute fool, and proven himself to be nothing more than a cad. Worse, an ignorant cad.

"It's getting light," said Anne unexpectedly.

Grateful for the excuse to look at her, Byron nodded. "Yes. Morning's here."

The carriage rumbled along. They were making good time— at least, that was what Campion had said. They had been away from the inn before dawn, and had continued for an hour or so before the sun's rays had started to peek through the window.

And in all that time, they had sat in silence.

Byron shifted wretchedly in his corner of the carriage. Well, what was there to say? He had proven himself to be the worst sort of man—one who would take advantage of a woman at the first opportunity.

And he had always considered himself better than that. Above that. Nobler, even.

After all, if a duke could not be trusted with a pretty woman, who could be?

"You should not worry so much, you know," came Anne's quiet words. "I have forgiven you."

Shame rushed to Byron's cheeks, and he was certain, even in this low light, she would see color pinking in them. "You have—I mean, you do?"

It seemed unlikely. Though he had met Miss Anne Mead just a few days ago now—*goodness, was it already a few days?*—she had never struck him as a woman who forgave easily. Though where he got that impression from, he was not sure.

Yet, she was looking at him with kind eyes. Far kinder than he deserved.

"It was a mistake, and one not to be repeated," she said, a little emphasis on the last word. "But a mistake nonetheless. I am not one to blame a man for a genuine mistake."

Relief, sweet and refreshing, crept across Byron's chest. "Truly?"

Slight embarrassment shone on Anne's own face. "You cannot be blamed for giving me what...what I asked."

Byron swallowed. Now that was a conversational direction he very much wished to pursue—but it would be a bad idea. He did not need to attempt it to know it.

Trapped as they were in this carriage, with space at a minimum and her delicate scent already intoxicating, Byron knew himself well enough to know if he talked about that kiss...well. It would not be the last one. He wouldn't be able to help himself, and he was almost sure she would welcome it again.

After all, she had asked him to kiss her while dreaming...

Byron quickly crossed his legs. *Blast.* That was the last thing he needed!

Anne carefully looked away through the window, though faint pink was spreading up her neck.

Oh, hang it all! Why did his body always have to betray him?

"I hope we are getting closer," he said aloud.

Anne's gaze snapped back to him. "I beg your—"

"To the mail coach!" Byron said hastily. Curse it all, even his words were betraying him! "I imagine we probably left before them, and we do not have the burden of nine people, only three."

There was a flicker of pain in Anne's eyes before she nodded and said quietly, "Yes, we shall have to hope we advance on them."

They fell into silence, but it was not the awkward, prickly silence they had suffered the day before. No, unless Byron was mistaken, this was rather...

Well. *Companionable.*

He had never experienced such a thing with a woman before. No, it was always his chums at the club who could sit with him in happy silence, each doing their own thing, each unconcerned by the presence of the other.

It was strange, actually, now that he came to think about it. Anne was about as far off from gentlemen like Dulverton as it was possible to be, and yet...

And yet Byron felt just as comfortable around her. Also, so on edge he hardly knew how to draw breath.

"So," Anne said quietly. "Who is in the mail coach for you?"

Byron frowned. The question did not make sense. *Who was in the mail coach?*

"It's...it's my sister," she said in a soft voice, gaze dropping to her hands. "My sister, Beth. In the mail coach."

Byron stared—and then it all came together.

"I placed my most precious possession on that mail coach."

He should have been more circumspect with his questioning!

Of course it was not a precious item, a valuable thing, in the mail coach that had driven Miss Anne Mead to accost a duke and demand he take her along with him on an adventure she did not even realize she was a part of.

No singular object could be worth that much—*at least*, he thought ruefully, *not one that someone would willingly place on something as precarious as a mail coach.*

No, it was a person. Her sister. That was why Anne was so determined to catch up with the mail coach—why she was so horrified to hear it was to be accosted by the Glasshand Gang.

"Everyone on that mail coach—they are in terrible danger!"

"Oh," said Byron helplessly. Dear God, she was magnificent. Not many sisters would risk so much and undertake such a treacherous journey for a sibling. "Younger sister, is she?"

Anne smiled mischievously, and the carriage warmed by several degrees. "Five years younger, and an absolute rascal, I'm afraid. I always promised her I would never let anything—it was supposed to be me."

Byron waited as the carriage jostled along. Anne's sentence did not entirely make sense, but he knew better than to interrupt. There was twisted distress on the woman's face, not taking away its beauty but revealing great inner turmoil.

"On the mail coach. I was meant to be the one traveling, but she insisted and—she can be rather persistent, Beth," said Anne dryly. "I am usually able to persuade her round to my style of thinking, but in this case—"

"She won," said Byron softly.

It was difficult not to be impressed—by both Mead sisters. Why, this Beth must have a will as strong as iron if she had been able to overcome the protestations of Anne. He had never met a woman with such fire, such determination.

Yet this Beth had won out?

"We are very close, Beth and I, and our brother," said Anne with a heavy sigh. "Perhaps I have indulged them, though I do not know what else I could...anyway. That is who is on the mail coach for me."

She affixed her gaze on him with a questioning look. Byron looked back at her, unsure precisely what she was expecting.

Praise, perhaps? He would dearly love to praise her. He had never met a woman with such loyalty to siblings, particularly as they had to be grown or near coming of age. And she would risk this all—not just the danger on the road, but her reputation. If anyone discovered that she and the Duke of Sedley had spent two nights on the road together, one in a carriage and one in a bedchamber...

"Do you have a sister? A brother?"

Byron's insides froze. "Why in God's name do you ask that?"

Instantly, he saw he had reacted too swift.

Anne was examining him with a raised eyebrow. "I did not think it was that strange a question."

And he supposed it wasn't. For most people. "I have no sister."

"So I suppose you think I have been foolish."

Byron looked up. "Foolish?"

"To rush about the place in search of my sister," said Anne with a dry smile. "I am sure there are many ladies of note whom you know that would not even consider running after such a foolish errand."

Byron grinned. "Perhaps not. But that does not signify that I believe the action to be a poor one."

She raised an eyebrow. "Do you mean to say you are impressed by me?"

Yes, he wanted to say. *Terribly impressed. Far more impressed than I thought I could be by a lady who has no title, wealth, or connections of any kind.*

If Anne had power, money, friends even, she could have gone to them and they would have helped her to retrieve her sister. *She evidently has none of those things, or why else stride into my carriage and demand I give her aid?*

She had no idea whose carriage she had stepped into, Byron could not help but think, and her love for her sister overcame all concerns. It was impressive. She was a woman who held to her friends and loved ones strongly, even in a dangerous situation.

Byron swallowed. But he could not permit her to know precisely how much he admired her. That would be a grave mistake.

And make those feelings all the more real.

"I am impressed, I suppose," he said aloud, as nonchalantly as possible. "There are few ladies who would risk so much, even for a sister."

"The thought of leaving Beth to her fate, to the Glasshand Gang...that I will not risk," said Anne with fierceness, her hands clenching into fists.

Byron felt such a kinship with her in that moment, it was hard to think. "That does you much credit."

Their eyes met and, for a moment, something dark and mysterious and giddy rushed through him. How could he explain it to her, this woman who thought of nothing save ruining her own reputation to save her sister? A woman who, despite his own misgivings, was turning out to be a rather pleasant road companion?

A woman who would undoubtedly visit his dreams in the coming nights...

"And what about you?" Anne prompted, interrupting his thoughts. "Who do you have on the mail coach?"

Byron stared. "I beg your pardon?"

She sighed with a wry shake of the head, and the thought that he wished to make her do that every day for the rest of his life flickered through his mind. And then it was gone.

And a good thing too, Byron told himself. In a few days, he would have caught up with the mail coach, brought the Glasshand Gang back to London, and returned to his stately existence as a duke.

And Anne...she would return to wherever it was that she came from.

"You have a loved one on the mail coach," Anne said clearly, as though trying to explain a triangle had three sides. "Why else would you charge after it after discovering the Glasshand Gang was going to attack it?"

It was a fair question, one Byron should have realized would, eventually, be asked. It was a great shame, therefore, that he had absolutely no answer prepared.

"Ah," he said aloud.

He would have to think quickly—and lie. It was something Byron hated to do, but he could see no way around it.

What was the alternative? Reveal he was a duke? Explain he sometimes worked closely with the authorities undercover to reveal miscreants? That he had, in fact, a personal history with the Glasshand Gang, which—

"My wife," Byron blurted out.

He cringed inwardly the instant the two words left his mouth, but it was too late. He could not take them back—and worse, he could not unsee the way Anne now looked at him.

"Your...your wife?" she said quietly. "I see."

What was he thinking? Byron knew it was a mistake to attempt to create a lie on the spot. He was always terrible at this sort of thing—it was the one reason Snee always said he would never amount to much when it came to helping out the justices!

And most irritatingly, he was right.

What must she think of him?

Byron did not need to guess. He could see. Anne's gaze flickered away, criticism unspoken yet resting in her gaze as she looked out the window.

She thought him some sort of rake, a man with no honor. A man who would race after one woman and yet kiss another.

Though it pained him greatly to see her distress—her disappointment in him—Byron was not sure what he could do. He had said the first thing that had come into his mind, and now to go back on that would make him out to be a liar.

And he was. Except she didn't have to know what kind of liar. *Oh, hang it all.*

"I mean my sister," Byron said hurriedly.

Anne looked back at him, a frown puckering her eyebrows, and he was suddenly reminded of that heady moment they had shared but a few hours before. Those kisses, willingly given by him and willingly, at the time, taken by Anne. The softness of her in his arms, the way her fingers had immediately curled into his hair. The way she had moaned at his touch...

But this was not the time to lose himself in the memories of a kiss which should not have been, Byron tried to tell himself. He sat here with a woman who once again thought him dishonorable, and somehow, he had to prove he was quite the opposite.

No one, he was sure, had been so ruled by honor as he was. Imprisoned by it.

"You mean your sister," Anne said slowly. "But you said wife. Which is it?"

It could not be more obvious that she was unimpressed by his response. Byron couldn't blame her. He wasn't feeling great about it himself.

The carriage rattled along the road, leaning slightly. Byron allowed himself to drift to the left, toward Anne. She did not move away.

Hope leapt in his heart, but it was immediately pushed aside by common sense. They were in a carriage, for goodness sake! Where could she go to escape him? That was no sign of her affection for him, and—

Byron caught himself just in time. *Affection?*

Now was not the time to be thinking of affection. In truth, he should not be thinking of it at all. He was not here to seduce Anne Mead, even if he wanted—

He had to catch up with that mail coach. Everything else was just distraction.

Thankful his manhood had quieted, Byron uncrossed his legs. "I meant my friend, who is like a sister to me...and the...the closest thing I have to a wife."

For a moment, his words hung in the air.

They sounded ridiculous, even to him. How he had managed to get himself in such a tangle, he did not know.

Well, that was not quite true. All Byron had to do was look up and see the pretty curve of her mouth, the tantalizing hint of beauty under the wrappings of her threadbare pelisse. Anne Mead was a woman who would tempt even a saint, and they hadn't had her in their arms, begging for a kiss.

Byron swallowed. "It's complicated."

"So I gather," said Anne, and then she laughed.

And what a laugh. Peals of giggles filled the carriage as all the tension started to ebb away. The merriment on her face made Byron smile despite himself. It was rather difficult not to smile when in the company of such a woman, particularly when she was so joyful.

"Oh, Byron, you can keep your secrets," she said eventually.

Byron's stomach lurched. Was that the first time she had used his name? It certainly was the first one he recalled, other than in her dream. Why did it do something so visceral to him, this intimacy he had never shared with another woman before?

"You—you do not mind if I call you Byron?" she said hesitantly, accurately reading the confusion on his face. "You did say—"

"I did, you are right," said Byron hastily. "Though, I admit, I did not expect you to."

For an instant, there was a teasing smile dancing across her face. There was something about Anne, Byron realized. Something hidden, squashed within her. Something she obviously fought to keep away from the gazes of others, yet something that, for brief moments, was visible.

A side of Anne he rather liked.

And then it was gone, and the serious expression he associated with her returned.

"Whether sister or wife or friend, I hope we reach the mail coach in time to save them," Anne said quietly. "I am not sure whether I will ever forgive myself if my sister came to harm."

Byron's stomach wrenched. Dear God, if only she knew…if

only she had any inkling just how he understood that fear.

"We will get there in time," he said stiffly. "To save all of them."

"But what if we—"

"We will," Byron insisted.

The thought of not succeeding was so abhorrent, he would not even permit it to be spoken. Once before, Byron had failed to stop the Glasshand Gang from committing a terrible crime, and he would never allow it to happen again. He had made that vow that horrible night. He would never go back on it.

"We are fortunate, I suppose, that we have your carriage," said Anne bracingly.

Byron looked up. Had she seen it—the pain on his face? Had he been too open, even if he had not spoken a word?

"Whatever hurt you carry with you, Byron, you do not have to share it with me," Anne said quietly, as though once again reading his mind. "As I am sure you can understand, there are plenty of things about myself that I have not...we are strangers, after all."

Byron's jaw tightened. "Strangers?"

"Just two people who share a similar goal, for now," said Anne in clipped tones, though her eyes were expressive. And then the warmth within them disappeared. "Once we reach the mail coach and save the people we care about, we will go on our separate ways."

It was on the tip of his tongue to say he had no desire to do that—go separate ways that was. That he wanted to know her better, to know the things about her she had not shared. To know, really know, Anne Mead.

Byron swallowed. "Of course. Separate ways."

CHAPTER EIGHT

September 7, 1810

NANCY COULD NOT help it. Even against her better judgment, when she was absolutely certain it was a bad idea, she...well. Fell into it.

It was his fault. Byron's. If he had not been such an interesting conversational partner, she never would have slipped into the habit of talking to him. But the roads were long, and the other sources of entertainment were lacking. Absent, in fact.

And so within an hour, Nancy found herself...conversing.

"Tell me something about yourself."

She almost grinned as Byron scrunched up his nose. "Dear lord, why?"

"Because I am bored, sir, and I require entertainment," Nancy quipped.

She did not understand it. How could a man so utterly devoid of charm in some ways be absolutely charming in others? Nancy had never met another man like him.

It was not as though Byron was attempting to attract her. He merely sat there, being jostled by the carriage as it meandered. He did not attempt to smile; he had not started the conversation. He had not even mentioned the searing kiss they had—

Anyway, Nancy thought. The point was, Byron was not attempting to seduce her, or anything untoward. Which made it all the more strange that she was drawn to him.

Not precisely like a moth to a flame. Like a deer, thirsty and tired, to water.

"And do you always require entertainment?" asked Byron with a raised eyebrow.

Nancy rolled her eyes. "Do not try to tell me ladies should supply the entertainment rather than be entertained themselves!"

"No, I was more thinking that, by the sound of it, you rarely had the opportunity to be entertained," he pointed out quietly. "It sounds to me as though you spend much of your life looking after that sister of yours."

Unable to prevent a smile from twisting her lips, Nancy nonetheless looked away. She could not deny it.

Most ladies of her acquaintance—at least, the ladies who admitted an acquaintance with the Mead family when they had been more affluent—were married now. Or if not married, at the very least, hostesses of repute. They hosted dinners, invited select guests to card parties, attended balls as envious eyes watched on.

She darned Matthew's socks and attempted to prevent Beth from ending up in the disreputable parts of London.

"It was you I was asking about," Nancy said to the window.

"Yet this is the role of conversation, to take us in unexpected turns, to surprise and delight," came Byron's voice.

She had to grin. "I suppose it is. I suppose your usual conversation partners offer something more impressive."

Try as she might, Nancy was unable to keep her curiosity from her voice.

Usual conversation partners.

Who were they? Who was this Byron Renwick? She'd never heard the name, which did not signify anything, but her father had been accustomed to mentioning many a-name when he had lived, and Renwick was not one she recognized.

What sort of man in business could simply decide to race

after a mail coach? What sort of man owned a carriage like this, stopped off at inns without asking the price of a room? A man with money, yes, but it was more than that. Nancy had watched him closely when they had arrived at each inn, and it hadn't even occurred to him to ask the price.

Who had so much money that even asking the cost was immaterial?

"You know, I know almost nothing about you," Nancy said aloud.

Byron appeared startled by her pronouncement. "Yes you do."

"No, I really don't," she said with a wry smile. "I know your name, and that you wish to capture the Glasshand Gang—"

"End them, more like," he muttered.

Nancy hesitated. There was something deep there, something she was certain he would not tell her. Despite her growing curiosity.

"Beyond that, I know nothing," she said aloud.

Byron shrugged. "I know almost nothing about you. We are strangers, I suppose."

Except, Nancy wanted to say as the carriage continued along the winding road, *I know you are an excellent kisser. That my whole body responds to you now, whether I like it or not. That each time you move, I am conscious of it, even if I am not looking at you. That—*

"You know a little about me," Nancy said hastily, trying to push away the indelicate thoughts that were invading her mind. It was not ladylike to think such things! "You know I have a sister, Beth."

Byron shrugged again. "You could be lying about her."

"I could be—why on earth would I lie about my sister?" Nancy said, startled.

It was a most curious accusation. No, not accusation; there was no malice or distrust in her companion's voice. She examined him closely, trying to ignore the way her stomach lurched as she took in his broad shoulders, the strong fingers clasped nonchalantly in his lap.

There was something more there.

And then it occurred to Nancy, as sparklingly strange as though a diamond had just fallen into her hands, that she *could* have lied. There was no reason to trust her, no evidence she could have given that she was a reliable soul.

And she had no evidence of that with him either.

Here they were, strangers, as he said. But they had to trust each other, did they not? *Or else, at the very least,* Nancy thought with a sigh, *it would be a very strange journey indeed.*

Even stranger than it already was.

"Fine," she said abruptly.

Byron had been gazing out the window during her reverie. "Fine?"

"Let's start again," said Nancy, inclining her head. "My name is Anne Mead."

He snorted, though there was teasing mischief in his eyes. "Seriously?"

"Come on, show willing," said Nancy briskly. It was the same tone she used with her brother whenever he was being difficult, and she was unsurprised to see it had precisely the same effect.

Byron rolled his eyes. "This is ridiculous."

"Oh, I am sorry, do you have somewhere better to be?"

He laughed. "I suppose not. Well then, I am Byron Renwick, as you well know."

He inclined his head, as though they had just been introduced at a ball.

Flutters of excitement soared through Nancy's chest. Which was foolish. This was just an odd game, something to pass the time. But it was pleasant, conversing with Byron like this. As though they were equals somehow. As though this was a genuine new meeting.

"I am the elder of three siblings, Beth and Matthew," said Nancy calmly. "And yourself? Do you have siblings?"

Now why did he hesitate? She could not understand it; it was not as though she was pressing him for familial secrets which should never see the light of day! *That was the way Beth would have put it*, Nancy thought dryly, and she could see her point.

All she had asked was whether Byron had siblings, and he hesitated. What secrets could there be in that quarter?

"And I," he said finally, "am an only child. Nancy, I don't see why—"

"My father was a gentleman, though sadly departed now, along with my mother," said Nancy briskly. She was determined to find out as much as possible about this man, and she was not going to take no for an answer. "I think you said you were in business?"

It was strange. Now that she came to think about it, the fact her father had been a gentleman and Byron was in trade should have meant that she was his social superior.

The idea jarred with her experience. No, Byron may be in business, but it was surely that sort of genteel business where no one really knew what it was, and within a generation his family could be called gentlemen. Byron did not give the impression of being in trade. Quite to the contrary, every inch of him screamed a gentleman.

Nancy swallowed. Amongst other things.

"I did," said Byron quietly.

"And that business is?"

"None of yours," he said with a wry smile. "Nancy Mead, why do you not just come out and ask what you want to know?"

Nancy flushed at the use of her nickname, but after all they had already shared, it seemed piquant to ask him to call her Anne. Or Miss Mead.

Because he was right. Goodness, he saw right through her; more's the pity.

Rain started to gently splatter onto the carriage, drumming on the roof and adding a warm cocoon feeling to the interior. Here they were, far from the rest of the civilized world. Anything could happen, Nancy could not help but think, and no one would ever know. She could be honest here, as bold as she often wished, but just as often censored herself.

"Fine," she said again. "What business are you in, Byron? Because I cannot think of anything that permits a man to just up and leave, if he is in trade—and you do not present yourself as a man in trade."

Byron raised a quizzical eyebrow. *Most irritating*, Nancy could not help but think. It even made him more handsome, and she had not thought that possible.

"Perhaps I am in a trade that requires me to travel."

"To Dover?" Nancy asked eagerly. "With no notice, with almost no possessions?"

"You have traveled without any," Byron pointed out.

She bit her lip. That much was true, and if she did not purchase another gown soon, she would scream. It was tiring of being in the same one for days at a time, and she was certain this floral pattern had faded greatly on the travels they had already taken.

"What is it you do?" she asked finally.

It was an uncouth way to ask, one that would have made her mother gasp in horror—but there was nothing for it. Only direct bluntness appeared to work with this man, and though Nancy colored, the words were said.

And Byron seemed to know instinctively just how much it worried her. He spoke with a teasing air. "Goodness, you are forthright, Miss Mead."

"Oh, don't give me that!" Nancy said, nudging his foot with hers just as she might do to her brother.

The response was totally different. Heat sparked up her foot at the most meager of contact, making it difficult to think of anything else other than the man seated opposite her.

It was a small carriage. Yes, that was why she suddenly felt so warm, Nancy tried to tell herself. That was why she felt as though the mere foot between them was no longer enough.

"I...help London," said Byron quietly.

Nancy's curiosity perked up. "Help London?"

The words did not make sense. How could one help a city? Unless one was a justice of the peace, perhaps, or a Parliamentarian. Otherwise, how could he—

"What do you mean?" she persisted. "Come on, Byron, I am hardly likely to tell anyone, am I?"

Nancy gestured around the carriage and tried not to notice just how close her fingers came to the man's chest. It really was a very small carriage, now that she came to think of it.

"Suffice to say that when London needs help, I provide it," he said effortlessly.

But that wasn't enough. *Needs help?* "You mean, chasing down criminals, like the Glasshand Gang? You work with the authorities to—"

"Something like that," Byron said with a considered shrug. "It is nothing."

It was very much not nothing, Nancy could tell. There was pride in that look that showed just how greatly the gentleman wished to speak of the services rendered—but he remained silent.

Discreet, she thought with a flicker of admiration. Now that was not something she could have predicted of Mr. Byron Renwick.

"And what about you?" Byron said quietly.

Nancy laughed. How could she help it? "Do not tell me you were raised in a barn, Mr. Renwick!"

For a moment, just a moment, the thunder she had seen returned, clouding his face. And then it was gone.

"What do you mean raised in a barn?" he said, his voice still a little hot. "I will have you know, I was raised by one of the best governesses in all—"

"Governess?" interrupted Nancy in curiosity.

Byron colored slightly. "Maybe."

There was so much he was holding back. So much about him he did not want her to know—which was unfathomable. There was no shame in having a governess. She'd had a governess. Why did he think that information worth hiding?

"I meant more, you do not seem abreast of current develop-ments," Nancy said slowly.

Byron's brows furrowed. "Current developments? I was not aware there were any current developments for women."

Nancy grinned. "I could not have put it better myself!"

For just a moment, a heady moment, she thought she had gone too far.

"Rights for women," her father had always groaned. "There has to be more to life than blithering on about rights for women, Nancy!"

Had she spoken out of turn? Would Byron be just as bored by her conversation as her father had always been?

And then he laughed. Byron's laughter filled the carriage, and it was a healing balm and a heady mixture of delight and desire, and Nancy bathed in it as though it was the warmest water from a volcanic spring.

At least, what she imagined water from a volcanic spring would be like.

"I suppose I deserved that," Byron chuckled as the carriage swerved to the left.

"Yes, you did," said Nancy with a quirk of a smile, her heart fluttering.

What was she supposed to do with her hands? She had never really thought about it before; her hands had just been...there. But now she was highly conscious of them, unsure whether they should be by her sides, or in her lap—and if in her lap, clasped or unclasped?

And why did they wish to reach out and grasp at the man who was simultaneously irritating and highly delightful?

"Yes, women get married, and have babies," Nancy said aloud, hoping that would distract her from the hand-location dilemma. "I believe that is all we are considered good for, which is a shame, for I think..."

Her voice trailed off.

No, this was not the time. It was rarely the time, Nancy thought darkly. She could even now hear Beth and Matthew's groans whenever she revisited the subject, particularly if she did so in public.

"No one wants to hear your complaining!"

"That's just the way it is, Nancy!"

Nancy swallowed. *For now*, she had always thought. One day, the world will be different for women. Surely it would?

"And you don't want to?"

Nancy started. Byron was waiting for her to respond, but she had absolutely no idea what he had said. "I beg your pardon?"

Byron grinned. "I said, you don't want to? Get married, I mean, and have children?"

And before she could answer like a rational human being, Nancy was overcome by a vision of something she absolutely should not be considering.

Children. Three of them, with her fiery red but Byron's sharp expression. One of them had his broad shoulders, another, her slight frame. And they were smiling, laughing, one of them snorting in a way that was most like her mother—

Nancy pushed the vision away as color tinged her cheeks, her stomach turning over.

Now was not the time to be thinking of her children—their children!

"Yes, I suppose I might," she said aloud, hoping to goodness Byron had not noticed the sudden interruption in their conversation. "But I do not wish for that to be the only thing."

She was suddenly conscious that the man seated opposite her was now somehow directly opposite. His knees were touching hers, each tiny movement of the carriage brushing them up against each other.

Nancy swallowed. This conversation had merely been designed to help her get to know the man, but all of a sudden, they appeared to have meandered into dangerous territory.

Matrimony? Children? How had she managed that?

"I think you are capable of many things, a mother being but one of them," said Byron quietly—so quietly Nancy was tempted to lean forward to hear him. "You are a woman, Nancy Mead, of many talents."

"I don't know what you mean," she said quietly. Yes, if she leaned forward, she would be able to—

"Well, you've captured my attention," Byron said in a low voice. "And that is something many women aim for, but none have succeeded."

Their eyes met and Nancy saw the attraction in his eyes. Or was that hers, reflected in his pupils? It was impossible to tell. Something was rushing between them, something she knew to be desire, but also knew she had to ignore.

"I don't know what you—"

"I think you do," he said quietly. "You can try to deny the attraction between us, Nancy. Try to dress it up in terms of getting to know each other, of finding out more about your companion on the road...but I think you know how I felt about you when I kissed you."

Nancy swallowed. She did. What she had not realized was just how much it had affected him—but she could see that now.

"I have a reputation to lose, but no dowry, and therefore, no prospects," she said quietly. "I suppose anything that happened in this carriage—"

"I would ask nothing of you that you did not wish to give."

It was impossible to concentrate as hidden and repressed desires Nancy had always tried to ignore flared up once again. Perhaps they would not have if the man before her was not so intoxicating. Irritating, yes. But devilishly handsome, too.

"Nancy," began Byron in a hushed voice.

He was unable to continue. The carriage jolted suddenly, and Nancy had been on the edge of her seat as it was. Thrust suddenly forward, she put out her hands to stop her fall, but they careered into something. Something warm yet hard as strong arms encircled her.

Byron. She had fallen into Byron.

Nancy looked up with wild eyes and saw her hands splayed against the man's chest, her buttocks in his lap, his hands clasped on her arms, keeping her steady.

And as she looked up into his eyes, she knew what he wanted. Knew what she wanted, deep within her. Knew she could say nothing, and nothing would ever be said by Byron, yet…

"We are going to have a great deal of time on the road, I think," Nancy whispered.

Byron nodded silently, his dark eyes affixed on hers.

She swallowed. *Well, why not?* She could spend her life arguing with her sister about the rights of women to demand what they wanted, but when she had the opportunity, she had to take it. Take him.

"You said you wouldn't kiss me unless I asked you to," she said hoarsely.

Byron swallowed hard, his Adam's apple bobbing. "I said I wouldn't touch you unless you asked me."

"Well, you've already broken that rule," Nancy pointed out.

"I don't see you in much of a hurry to leave my arms."

She had to smile. "I suppose not. I…I haven't been able to stop thinking about that kiss, you know."

And Byron groaned, his hands tightening on her arms for just a moment. "Don't tempt me unless you're going to—"

Nancy leaned forward, unsure of how but certain she knew what she wanted.

Their lips touched. Warm spread through her toes as pleasure flickered through her, and Nancy gave herself up to the embrace and warm kisses of Byron Renwick.

CHAPTER NINE

B YRON GROANED. "WHAT do you mean we have to stop?"
Stopping was a problem. It had been ever since Nancy
had launched herself into his arms, and they could no longer hide
from the desire blossoming between them.

How long had it been since they had started kissing? A minute? An hour?

"And I am telling you, if we do not stop at this town and find
me another gown, I am going to—"

"Take it off?" said Byron hopefully.

He had been unable to help himself, but was well rewarded
for his boldness. The delicate shade of pink coating Nancy's
cheeks as he trailed kisses down her neck was instantly replaced
by a sharper shade of red. It highlighted her lips perfectly.

Byron tried not to groan. He was swimming in dangerous
waters here, he knew. Nancy was...was everything. Was nothing.
Was a no one, and yet had become someone.

Ah, hang. He had to untangle all this before they reached
Dover...

"Absolutely not!" Nancy said, removing herself from his lap
and sitting primly on the other side of the carriage.

Byron sighed. *Well, it had been a rather long shot.* "You really
feel the need for it? I mean, the mail coach is surely just ahead of

EMILY E K MURDOCH

us—if we can—"

But he was prevented from continuing by Campion, whose face had appeared. "Hullo, sir," he said with a grin.

Byron repressed one of his own. That was the trouble with permitting one's servants to lose some airs and graces required when speaking to a duke. They all of a sudden had ideas above their station.

Even though it was rather amusing.

"Yes, Campion?"

"Toll road ahead, sir," said his driver promptly. "It's new; I'd say the mail coach has probably gone around. Taken the longer route."

Bryon perked up immediately. "The longer route?"

This was perfect—precisely what he needed. They had been chasing the mail coach every step of the way, always behind, never quite closing the gap. But if the mail coach had taken a longer route, it was simple. They could take the toll road, and—

"Is there a town nearby, Campion?" said Nancy, inconsiderately interrupting Byron's thoughts. "One with a dressmaker, perhaps?"

Byron rolled his eyes. "Your gown is fine!"

More than fine. The more he looked at it, the more he noticed just how elegant the cut was, how it subtly emphasized every curve and swell of her body. There was absolutely nothing wrong with it. Not something a few careful fingers undoing ribbons could not improve...

Nancy shot him a glare. "I came without luggage because time was absolutely of the essence to catch the Glasshand Gang—"

"And still is!" Byron pointed out.

Not that he had any experience of getting ladies out of gowns. He bit his lip. They looked to be most complicated things. More ribbons and ties than he knew what to do with, and a few buttons on the side. Why would they make them so complicated? They were designed to be removed, weren't they?

"A short break in whatever town is close by to purchase a

new gown will still leave us ahead," Nancy pointed out.

Byron swallowed his thought that if they did not stop, they would be even further ahead.

He was becoming blinded, he knew, by his fierce devotion to the vow he had made. The Glasshand Gang would be brought to justice. If it was the last thing he did, they would pay for what they had done.

But he wasn't so foolish as to think he could out-argue Nancy Mead. She was glaring with such ferocity, he was surprised his cravat had not burst into flames.

"Byron Renwick, I need another gown," she said sternly. "We won't catch them today; it will have to be tomorrow, but I'll be blowed if I spend another day in this—"

"Fine, fine," he said hastily, raising his hands in mock surrender. "Far be it for me to argue with you."

He caught her eye and had to work hard not to smile. Campion was still peering in as the carriage rattled along, and the last thing he needed was for a servant to guess at the intimacy he and his traveling companion had...well. Slipped into.

Not that it was enough. Oh, every kiss seared her name onto his heart and Byron was finding it more and more difficult to remind himself that once the Glasshand Gang was caught, Nancy would be reunited with her sister and that would be the end of it. Their acquaintance, if that was what they could call it, would be over.

"So we are stopping then?"

"We are indeed," said Byron with a hearty sigh.

Nancy beamed. "Thank you, Campion."

Her prim voice told the servant in no uncertain terms that they wished to be alone, and Byron could not help but be impressed. She may not be the wealthy, titled lady of the sort he most often met, but she had far more class.

"Don't be angry."

Byron looked up. Nancy was examining him with an expression he could not entirely read. She was not afraid, but she was concerned.

Concerned for him?

"I don't know what you mean," said Byron stiffly, shuffling awkwardly in his seat.

But Nancy did not look away. "You know precisely what I mean. You are angry, frustrated perhaps, that we have not caught the Glasshand Gang yet. But we will."

Somehow, there was such certainty in her voice, Byron found it hard to imagine how he could ever disagree with her. Which was a problem. He wasn't here to be seducing young ladies, true, but he also wasn't here to be seduced by them!

"And I really do need a gown," said Nancy, just a hint of pleading in her tones. "You would not deny me the comfort of refreshing my attire, would you?"

Byron cleared his throat. There were many things he wished to do to Nancy's attire, but replace it with another that would just as sufficiently cover the soft delight he felt whenever she was in his arms? That was one of them.

"A short visit then," he said gruffly, pushing away the desires he must ignore. "And then back on the road."

Nancy kissed him on the cheek, and Byron fought the impulse to bring his hand to where her lips had brushed his skin. "Thank you."

Byron snorted. It seemed the safest thing to do. If he even thought about opening his mouth, he was liable to spill all his secrets. All his yearnings.

And that would never do.

The carriage pulled up about ten minutes later on a street unfamiliar to Byron's eyes. They all looked the same outside of London.

"Oh, that feels good," Nancy groaned as she was helped out of the carriage by Campion.

Byron shot him a look, and the servant grinned. He had almost made it in time to help the beautiful woman out, but again, his driver had beaten him to it. *Drat him.*

"You never realize just how folded up you are in a carriage until you spend five hours within it," Nancy remarked with a dazzling smile as Byron offered her his arm.

"I did not think the time was spent that unpleasantly," he said under his breath.

He felt as well as saw her flush. With her hand tucked into his arm, Byron could feel the heat rushing through her, the heady reminder of the kisses they had shared as the carriage had rumbled by, keeping their secret for them.

"I suppose not," said Nancy with a grin as they started to walk down the provincial street. "But as we will not be catching up with the mail coach today, we will not lose much time if we stroll about for half an hour or so."

"Half an—"

"We'll just purchase a gown, obviously," she continued, cutting across him with a mischievous grin. "Are you really going to attempt to say no to me?"

Byron opened his mouth, made a bizarre sort of strangled sound, cursed himself for being a complete fool, and closed it again.

Well, he had not expected this.

Ladies always attempted to attract the attention of a duke; it appeared to be something bred into them at the bone level. Byron had understood it, too, up to a point. After all, he would be callous indeed to pretend he didn't know he was an excellent match.

In fact, now that Dulverton was married, there were few eligible bachelors such as him. The entire *ton* knew it, especially the mamas. It was an unusual day indeed if Byron could walk the streets of London without young ladies being almost literally thrown at him.

Dropping handkerchiefs had become commonplace. One young miss had actually launched herself into the street, expecting him to rescue her. The trouble was, as Byron had attempted to explain to her hysterical father later, he had been looking into a shop window at a particularly fine set of pistols and had been entirely ignorant of the young lady's attempt to gain his attention.

It had been a broken wrist only, apparently. Byron had paid Dr. Walsingham with bad grace, and studiously avoided the family ever since.

"Byron?"

Byron blinked. He was no longer walking. When had he stopped walking?

"You got lost there," Nancy said conversationally. "Where were you?"

Not somewhere he wanted to explain, he thought darkly. He had been tempted, earlier that day when Nancy had been so insistent to learn all about him, merely to tell her. But how could he put it?

"Actually, I'm a duke. Yes, a duke. The technical term is 'Your Grace'. No, I don't..."

"Yes, I'm a duke, but I also have a deep familial secret I carry with me like a heavy dark burden and can never reveal..."

"Yes being a duke is impressive, but once I bring the Glasshand Gang to justice..."

Byron smiled wanly. No, none of those would do.

He blinked. They were standing outside a modiste.

"Oh, hell," he said weakly.

"It won't take long to find what I need," said Nancy promptly, pulling him up the steps and opening the door. A bell jangled. "Ooooh!"

Byron groaned. That was precisely what he had been afraid of.

Not having a sister, he had never spent much time in a modiste's, but he had heard sufficient horror stories from the married men at the Dulverton Club to be prepared for the nonsense he was about to suffer.

If anything, it had not adequately prepared him. More's the pity.

"Ah, Madam, your husband wishes to treat you to a new set of gowns and underclothes?" simpered a woman who appeared as though by magic from behind a screen.

Byron swallowed. The thought of purchasing underclothes for Nancy was doing very uncomfortable things to his body, and he could not allow the misunderstanding to continue. *Even if—no. No!*

"Actually, no, I—"

"My husband will be purchasing one gown for me only," said Nancy smoothly, squeezing her hand on his arm firmly.

Byron almost swallowed his own tongue as he simultaneously attempted to speak and halt his words. Husband? Why did his whole body quiver to hear that word from her tongue?

But then, he supposed as he was relegated to sitting in an armchair and Nancy was taken over to the fabric lying in racks to his left, he had done much the same thing to her last night at the inn. It was only fair she utilize the same falsehood to maintain their respectability.

Even if it made him want to…oh, demand things a husband was owed.

Stoically, Byron once again crossed his legs. It was her fault he had to make a habit of this.

"But the thing is, we need a gown today," Nancy was saying.

The modiste raised an eyebrow. "Today?"

Byron held his breath. It was unusual; all gowns, as far as he was aware, were like jackets, waistcoats, breeches. They were made to measure, each elegantly constructed for one person. A specific person. One could just as easily wear another man's boots as put on his waistcoat in comfort.

And if gowns were the same, it was certainly not going to be a quick stop. No, they would be there for hours, if not days. And with each passing moment, the mail coach—

"That is a shame," said Nancy elegantly with a genteel shake of her head. "I had supposed you may have a gown or two you use as a sample which you could be…persuaded, I think, to part with."

Byron tried not to smile. If he had ever needed a demonstration that Nancy had indeed been born a gentleman's daughter, this was it. The refinement with which she spoke, the delicate choice of words, the effortless modulation of her voice.

It was impossible not to be impressed. How did she do it, this woman who was so impulsive as to agree—nay, demand—to travel with him? How did she surprise him at every turn? It was most disagreeable.

And wonderful.

"I think I may have just the thing," the modiste said. "If Madam would mind stepping behind the screen, we may begin the fitting."

Byron's mouth went dry. "Oh, uh, right. I can wait out—"

"You do not mind if my husband remains in the shop, do you?" Nancy asked sweetly, widening her eyes at Byron as though attempting to communicate something.

She could not be serious! He could not remain here while her gown was removed just feet away from—

"Oh, that is quite acceptable," said the modiste breezily as she returned with a cream silk gown with a red-and-green floral pattern. "You are quite happy there, aren't you, sir?"

Byron stared wide eyed as Nancy stepped behind the screen. The sound of buttons undoing and ribbon unfolding drifted over it.

"F-Fine," he breathed, hardly knowing what to do with himself.

Dear lord, what fresh hell was this? The knowledge that Nancy was just behind that screen, behind a few feet of wood and silk, removing...Byron forced himself to stay seated. Removing her gown?

"I do not require any assistance," came Nancy's calm voice from behind the screen. "Would you mind leaving us as we discuss the gown?"

Byron's mouth went dry. *Oh, no.* At the very least, the modiste could act as a sort of chaperone, even if she would not know it. But with her gone...

"You are very quiet."

Byron cleared his throat not once, but twice. His voice was still weak when he eventually spoke. "I-I am?"

"You do know I am going to have to ask you to pay for this?" came Nancy's voice, hesitant now. "I have no coin with me."

Byron nodded, then realized she could not see him. "That's fine."

"Good," said Nancy's voice. "There we go."

The gown she had been wearing since the moment he had first met her was suddenly thrown over the screen, proving the woman behind it was...

He could not help it. He groaned.

Oh, the temptation to just rise and step around that screen...to see Nancy in all her finery. Her true finery. This was not a woman who needed fine silks or jewels to be beautiful, she managed that all by herself.

"Byron?"

"Nancy," he gasped as her head appeared around the screen. Dear lord, she was almost completely nude behind there...

"Are you quite well?" Nancy said, concern clouding her expression. "You sounded in pain for a moment there."

Byron tried to smile. In pain? She had no idea. "Quite fine, I assure you—now get that gown on, quickly."

"Quickly?" she asked, though her head disappeared once more behind the screen.

Yes, he wanted to say. *For my own sanity.* "We must be on the road as swiftly as possible. I still wish to catch the mail coach today."

"I suppose we must try," came Nancy's voice as the sound of silk rustling over skin met his ears. "The idea of anything happening to my sister..."

It was impossible to tell whether her voice had halted due to her fear for her sister, or whether she was tackling a rather difficult ribbon. Byron tried not to think about how he could offer to help her, and instead spoke of the first thing that popped into his mind.

"You are going to a great deal of trouble for your sister. What about your brother?"

"What about him?"

Byron shrugged. "Well, you led me to believe—"

"You say that like I've been lying to you," came Nancy's teasing voice.

He had. And worse, Byron knew that of the two of them, he was the one who had been lying. Well, hiding the truth. It amounted to the same thing.

"I was going to say, you have shared how much you care for both your siblings," he said aloud. "But what of your brother? Does he remain in London to fend for himself?"

Byron had attempted a jocular tone, but the silence that followed seemed to lengthen uncomfortably until, finally, Nancy broke it. The moment she had, he wished she hadn't.

"No, he's not in London," she said quietly, the sound of a ribbon bow being tied accompanying her words. "He's missing. In France. He's a soldier."

Byron closed his eyes for a moment. Damn him, and his curious tongue!

"I am sorry."

"Don't be, it is not your fault," came Nancy's airy voice, which only highlighted how pained she truly was. "But with no parents, Matthew is very much my responsibility."

"I would have thought you would be his," Byron inquired.

Nancy poked her head around the screen, and though her eyes glistened, no tears had been shed. "Why, because I am a woman?"

"Well..." Byron said awkwardly.

Yes. But somehow that was not precisely the right answer to give.

"I have to look after them," Nancy said sternly before disappearing back behind the screen. "I always have, and I always will. I made a vow."

Byron could not help but chuckle. "Goodness, you sound like me."

"You?"

"I made a vow once," he said, the words spilling from his lips despite himself. "A vow to...well, it has led me to look after a great number of people, most of whom will never know I have cared for them."

That was the challenge and the reward of the life they lived, Snee had once said. You serve, and you try your best. And no one ever thanks you.

"But then in that case," said Nancy, sweeping out in silk, "who looks after you?"

Byron's mouth fell open.

There was no other response. She looked absolutely beautiful, stunning, with her red hair a perfect contrast to the shimmering cream-and-green gown. The delicate stitching was so minute, the gown appeared to have been created through magic. It fit her perfectly.

It made him want to rip the damned thing off her.

"I said," Nancy said quietly. "Who looks after you?"

Byron met her gaze and forced down the response he wished to give: that he hoped, perhaps, it could be her.

A foolish thought. In a day or two, their business would be complete and he would have no reason to see Nancy again. He could not forget that.

"I'll buy the gown," Byron said, voice dry. "Then we had better get back on the road."

CHAPTER TEN

THERE WAS A strange sort of tension in the carriage, and Nancy did not know what to do about it.

It had started…when they were at the modiste? But that had felt different, Nancy thought as the carriage continued onward and she tried not to look at Byron's face, which was impassive.

There had been tension there, yes, but of an entirely different kind.

This was new. The closer they approached the next stop, the more the tension built between them. Well, perhaps not between them exactly. Around them. In the carriage as it trundled forward to the town Campion was sure the mail coach would be stopping at that night.

In just a few hours, perhaps less, the journey would be over.

Nancy swallowed. She wasn't supposed to feel sad about it. The only reason she had even spoken to Byron in the first place was to protect her sister.

"Everyone on that mail coach—they are in terrible danger!"

Allowing Beth to get onto that mail coach had been a mistake, and she should have known it—but she hadn't. This was her opportunity to rescue her.

So why did the thought of finally catching up with the Dover mail coach—particularly before the Glasshand Gang reached it—

fill her with such sadness?

"Almost there."

Nancy blinked. Byron's words were sharp, short. The horrible tension coursing through her body pulsed.

"Almost there."

What would she do once they found it? Once Beth was safe in her arms, and whoever it was that Byron was chasing after was safe in his?

A red-hot jealousy such as Nancy had never known almost overcame her. The thought slipped into her mind, scalding, that this entire time, Byron had not been coming on this journey to spend more time with her. Far from it. He was chasing after someone of his own, someone who evidently meant a great deal to him.

And she had allowed him to kiss her. Kiss her furiously. They had clung together. She had wanted it, craved him, wanted more...

But all that would be over in mere minutes.

Nancy swallowed, trying to ignore the disappointment curdling in her stomach. She was being ridiculous, but...this whole situation was so unusual. She had never done anything like this before, never been so bold, so inconsiderate of the consequences.

Within the hour, she would be saying her goodbyes to Byron Renwick.

"You look troubled."

Nancy tried to smile, but she'd never been much good at hiding her emotions. "I do?"

Byron nodded with a quiet smile. "I am beginning to learn the contours of your face, Nancy, and that particular expression is not a joyful one."

Heat seared her cheeks. He was learning the contours of her face?

It was not such a scandalous thing to say...except it was. It spoke of attention, and interest, and the attraction between them Nancy hadn't spoken of but he certainly had.

"You can try to deny the attraction between us, Nancy. Try to dress it up in terms of getting to know each other, of finding out more about your companion on the road...but I think you know how I felt about you when I kissed you."

Nancy swallowed. All this heat between them, it felt as though it should go somewhere—but where?

Byron was entangled with someone else, she told herself firmly. That was to be expected. A man like that, looking like that, as charming as that, with money...

Well, it was no wonder he was married. Or whatever he was.

And once she had Beth safe, they could return to London—precisely how, she was not sure—and that would be the end of the matter. She would never see Byron again. Never think of him. Probably.

"Nancy," said Byron urgently, suddenly leaning forward.

Nancy's heart leapt. "Yes?"

"I—"

"Here we are!"

Nancy started. She had not noticed Campion's face appearing, but his triumphant laugh was jarring. Disappointment flowed through her as Byron leaned back, evidently no longer willing to speak.

Or able.

What had he been about to say? Nancy's mind whirled with the possibilities as the carriage began to slow. Had he wished to say how much he cared? No, that would be ridiculous. Perhaps he wanted to say how much he had enjoyed their time together. Or how he would miss her. Or—

"Here we are," the driver repeated with delight, slowing the carriage to a stop. "Goodness, I thought we'd never get here."

And neither did I, Nancy wanted to say sadly. *But now, we are here...*

It was foolish of her, selfish of her to wish the journey could continue. She was supposed to be rescuing Beth from the Glasshand Gang. That was far more important than any sort of foolish flirtation with a gentleman who had still told her almost nothing about himself.

But as Byron swiftly left the carriage on one side and stepped around to help her out from the other, Nancy could not ignore the tingle of his fingers on hers. It was the first time he had helped her down, and she should not see anything more in the gesture than common politeness, she was sure.

Even though she wanted to...

"Well," Nancy said briskly, releasing her hand from Byron's, as he seemed in no hurry to do so. "Here we are. And this is where—"

"This is where the mail coach will be stopping for tonight," said Campion with a nod. "If you will excuse me, Miss, *Sir*, I'll go and inquire."

Perhaps it was her imagination, but Nancy could not help but think there was a knowing or teasing look between the two men as the driver stepped away.

As though there was a secret between them, one to which she was not privy to.

But that was surely her imagination. It was all this excitement about the Glasshand Gang, she told herself. She was seeing mystery where there simply wasn't any.

"So," she said bracingly.

Byron smiled as he stood beside her. "So."

Nancy swallowed. She had not intended to be standing quite so close to the tall man. But it would be churlish to step away, wouldn't it?

Besides, she did not wish to. It was rather pleasant, in this chilly autumnal breeze, to have him protecting her from the cold. At least, that was what she could argue if challenged.

"Your adventure is coming to an end."

Nancy tried to smile. "I suppose it is."

"I have greatly enjoyed your companionship," said Byron quietly. His dark eyes appeared deeper somehow. "It would have been a dull journey indeed without you."

She tried to nod. It was better than attempting to speak. What could she say? That she had never felt more alive than when with him? That her entire life had been dull, caring for others and never doing a thing for herself, until she had met him?

"Kiss me."

That she would never be able to forget the way his lips seared hers, pressing promises unspoken and unbidden onto her mouth? How she wanted to ask him more, to ask him to choose her and not the woman who was on the mail coach—

"What will you do?"

"When?" Nancy said hurriedly, forced from her reverie.

Byron smiled. "When you have your sister."

"Oh." It was on obvious question. "We shall return to London, I suppose. Or Dover, if we can find our way there safely."

"Dover?"

Nancy nodded with a wry smile. "You forget, I have two troublesome siblings, not one. Having to rescue both of them from themselves is not a pleasant business, but must be done."

For a moment, Byron just stared—then his mouth fell open. "You do not seriously intend to go to—you would not go to France?"

"Why not?" replied Nancy, pulling her pelisse around her and trying to speak far more confidently than she felt. "He is my brother, and—"

"He should be the one protecting you!" said Byron with an astonished expression. "Nancy, you are—you are precious! You cannot be risking yourself for—"

"Just for my brother?" Nancy said, trying and failing to ignore the word "precious." *She was precious?*

"Nancy Mead, I do not want you going to France and risking your life for a man," Byron said firmly, stepping toward her. He did not really need to; there had only been a foot between them as it was. Now it was a few inches. "You must promise me you will not do anything so rash."

Nancy looked into the eyes of the gentleman who had been

impossible to understand from the moment she had met him.

Equal parts charming, infuriating, and dazzlingly handsome, she never quite knew what to do with him. Each moment he spoke, he surprised her. Each time she thought she understood him, she was proven wrong.

"I cannot do it," she whispered, unable to look away. "I cannot give you my word when I know I shall break it."

"Damn it, woman!" breathed Byron darkly, lowering his head in frustration.

Nancy could not honestly say she was sorry. It brought him closer, and every moment they could share together like this was...what she wanted. All she wanted.

"Nancy Mead," came his voice, low and full of passion. "If you do not give me your word, I will pick you up bodily and—"

"It's not here."

Both Nancy and Byron whirled around, her heart racing at the thought of what he had been about to say. Would he really do such a thing? Pick her up in the middle of an inn's yard and place her back within his carriage?

It would be outrageous. It would be scandalous. It would be delicious.

But she could not think on that now. Campion was standing before them, pulling his hand through his hair in evident distress.

"It's not here."

"What do you mean it's not here?" Byron said urgently.

But Nancy did not need further explanation. She could see the truth on the man's face. "The mail coach. It's not here."

"What the—"

"The innkeeper said they had expected it an hour ago, but it never came," gabbled Campion. "And two other coachmen said they had seen it take the Ashford road—"

"Goddamnit!"

Nancy started. Byron had stepped away and swung his fist as though approaching an attacker. His hand rushed through the air, the movement creating a rushing sound.

There was such agony on his face, Nancy's heart skipped a beat. This wasn't just the frustration of a disappointed man. This was someone who had pinned a great deal of his happiness—or sanity—on something that had not occurred.

"Blast them all to hell, where are they going?" Byron exploded. "The Ashford road?"

"It's a far longer route, not one I would ever have recommended," Campion continued, looking greatly concerned at Byron's distress. "Perhaps they have been warned—perhaps they seek to avoid the Glasshand Gang by—"

"Then they are fools, leaving the trusted roads and venturing off somewhere on their own!" Byron said, fury still in his voice, but his tones started to calm. "Lord, how can I protect them if they do not—"

"We could leave now, but it would be impossible to catch them without knowing which route they are taking," said his driver urgently. "I could wait, ask other drivers..."

Nancy was suddenly conscious she was no longer a part of the conversation. Oh, she was still standing right beside Byron. She could feel the anger radiating from him like heat.

But she was utterly ignored. He and Campion whispered urgently, attempting to decide on the best course of action.

Her heart was thundering in her chest and she tried to breathe slowly to calm it.

So, the mail coach had taken a different road. Did that mean they were forewarned? Would that be enough? Would Beth be safe?

"—getting dark," Campion was saying.

"I don't care! We'll drive through the night if we have to!" Byron replied angrily.

Nancy watched as the driver hesitated. There was evidently great respect between them—but Byron was the master, and Campion the servant.

"The horses are exhausted," the driver said eventually, stepping back as though concerned Byron would start swinging fists again. "We have to rest. If we are going to catch them tomor-row—"

"We must—"

"Your man speaks sense," said Nancy quietly.

She flushed as both men turned to her. The curiosity of the servant's gaze was nothing to the intensity of his master's.

"Think, Byron—just think, for a moment," she said urgently. "We both wish to catch that mail coach and prevent the Glasshand Gang from harming anyone. That means we must think of the practicalities."

Byron waved an irritable hand. "I don't want to think of the—"

"I know, and that is one of the many differences between us," Nancy said with a wry smile. "You evidently never had to."

He glared. "And what does that mean?"

"Only that when one falls from relative wealth into relative poverty, one has to learn how to make do and mend," Nancy said steadily, not permitting the ferocity of his glare to overcome her. "I have learned to spot opportunities and leverage them—and know when I need to halt and regroup. There is no point losing ourselves in the Kentish countryside in the dark."

Her breath was short, but Nancy knew she spoke sense. Whether or not the man she was speaking to was the most handsome creature she had ever seen, she was the one with the right idea here, not him.

Barreling off into the dark, with brow-beaten horses and no idea where they were going? Madness.

"Leave us," muttered Byron.

Nancy swallowed. It was unpleasant to be so dismissed, but then, she supposed, she was a woman. How many women made decisions when there were two men involved?

But she had only taken two steps toward the carriage when a hand grabbed hers.

"Not you," Byron said quietly. "Campion, see to the horses."

Nancy stared as the servant was dismissed and she remained with Byron outside the inn. His hand was still on hers. His touch burned her, but it ignited a fire far deeper.

A fire she had to ignore.

"You are right," said Byron in an undertone.

Her lips quirked. "I beg your pardon?"

"I said, you are right," Byron repeated, a teasing look on his face. "You really had to make me say it again, didn't you?"

"I will always demand compliments from you are repeated at least twice," said Nancy with a laugh, excitement rushing through her.

Why did his admission feel like such a compliment? Why did a few civil words from him make her feel as though she was the most beautiful, most important woman in the world?

"I don't want to stay here, but I can see we have no real choice," Byron was saying with a heavy sigh. "It's another night on the road when I would rather be bringing the Glasshand Gang to their knees, but..."

Nancy did not think. She merely acted on instinct.

Well, perhaps not instinct. Perhaps it was easy to do this, standing beside such a handsome man, his fingers intertwined with hers.

She squeezed his hand. "It's the right decision. Well. The least wrong one, I suppose."

He grinned. "Well, the question is, are you willing to go all the way?"

Nancy dropped his hand as though she had been scalded. "I beg your pardon?"

What on earth had possessed him to say such a thing—even think it? Yes, they had shared some kisses, some rather delightful kisses. But that did not mean she was about to offer him everything that made her honorable in the eyes of society!

"Nancy," Byron began.

"I do not know where you got such an idea," said Nancy blanching as he tried to reach out for her, fully aware of where he had received such an idea.

"Kiss me, Byron."

"But I am not—"

"I meant," said Byron firmly, speaking over her, "all the way across Kent. To find them. The mail coach."

Oh. Well, that did make far more sense. "Oh," Nancy said helplessly.

There was a far too knowing look on the gentleman's face. If she did not know any better, she would think he rather delighted in teasing her. *The scoundrel.*

What a shame she liked the scoundrel so much.

"We should still be in time to save all nine of them," Byron was saying, "but only if you are willing to do whatever it takes."

Nancy nodded, swallowing her questions.

Who was she, this woman of his on the mail coach? Had ever a gentleman risked so much to save her? Was it a romantic connection—was she just making a fool of herself with Byron as he raced after a woman he loved while kissing her?

Or was it truly a sister? Was this adventure far more similar for them both than she had initially thought?

"I am willing," Nancy breathed.

Traveling with Byron, even if it meant chasing after his paramour, was an opportunity she simply could not abandon. Though she would undoubtedly have the rest of her life to cherish the few scant memories they would make together, they would burn brightly in her mind. Special moments. Moments she did not want to lose.

"So," Nancy said aloud, trying not to think of how deeply she was starting to care for him. "What do we do now?"

Byron sighed and jerked his head at the inn. "Keep going tomorrow. Spend the night."

Nancy smiled weakly. "I suppose we will have to hope they have more than one bed."

CHAPTER ELEVEN

September 8, 1810

"OH, YE GODS, I think I'm broken," moaned Byron, eyes still shut.

There was a muffled laugh from somewhere to his left, but he couldn't see. Partly because his eyes were shut, but that wasn't the only reason. All he could see from this vantage point was the end of the very large four-poster bed in the inn's last bedchamber.

A very large four-poster bed that would have been perfect for his aching back, his sore behind, and a rather uncomfortable twist he apparently now had in his neck.

This was ridiculous. He wasn't...getting old, was he?

"Broken?" came a soft voice.

Byron did not answer. At least, not with words. He groaned as he tried to sit up, bones protesting every inch of movement.

"I should have known this was a bad idea," he said with a sigh, swinging his legs over the edge of the sofa and trying to stretch out his arms. "This damned—sorry, this dratted—"

"Oh, please don't apologize for cursing," said Nancy airily, propping herself up on a pair of what appeared to Byron to be luxurious cushions. "My brother turns the walls blue if he stubs his toe, and he's not a particularly coordinated chap."

Byron bit down the questions that flooded into his mind at this revelation. Particularly the ones about sending uncoordinated youngsters into battle.

"Still, you are a lady," he said awkwardly, averting his gaze.

It was not that Nancy was improperly dressed. At least, she wouldn't be for a normal bedchamber.

It was more the fact that he was in it. Looking at her. Seeing her when she had just arisen, lips plump, eyes still waking up to the slow dawning light outside.

Light outside?

"We had better get a move on," said Byron hastily, rising swiftly.

He quickly collapsed back onto the sofa with a groan, holding his side. He would simply have to see Dr. Walsingham as soon as he got home, that was all. If he was ever to walk properly again.

Who would have thought sleeping on a sofa could be so torturous to the back?

"You had better close your eyes," said Nancy, warning in her tone as she pushed back the bedclothes.

Byron obeyed immediately, though under a silent protest. The last thing he wanted to do was miss the opportunity to see more of Nancy than he had already felt...

They had not talked about it. The bubbling, heightened attraction that lay between them. At least, he had tried. Almost.

"You can try to deny the attraction between us, Nancy...but I think you know how I felt about you when I kissed you."

But beyond that, they had allowed themselves about an hour of kissing in the carriage as though that would get it out of their system, then tried, so far successfully, to keep their hands to themselves.

Byron almost moaned as silk swished past him, just out of reach of his fingertips.

It was torment, having her so close yet out of reach. But that was only right, after all. She was a lady. He was a gentleman— more than a gentleman, a duke.

It was easy to forget that out here on the road.

"You're not looking?"

Byron swallowed, his mouth dry. "I wouldn't dare."

The truth was, he would dare—if it was anyone else. Merely a woman he had met, a lady he had just been introduced to. Someone who did not matter.

But Nancy mattered. There was something about her, something that drew him. He could not help but admire her. Most ladies, as far as he could tell, were far more interested in music, gossip, and sweet confectionery than anything approaching common sense.

Nancy appeared to be made entirely of common sense. Common sense and elegance.

Byron swallowed. His fingers were tingling as he heard Nancy move about the room. What could she possibly be doing that would require so much movement yet so much silence? The temptation to open his eyes, rise and surprise her, pull her into his arms and—

"There," came Nancy's voice from far too close. "I am presentable."

Byron slowly opened his eyes, expecting at any moment to be castigated for doing so.

"Arghhh," he managed.

That was all he could say. What else was he supposed to say? It was most unfair that Nancy could look like that when she had slept in what he could only assume was a subpar bed after an exhausting day.

She looked...perfect. As though about to step into Almack's and dazzle with a dance. As though she had just laid down a royal flush at Lady Romeril's card party, upsetting both the hostess and whoever was at her table.

Byron's stomach twisted painfully as his heart skipped a beat.

It was a good thing he was far too focused on the Glasshand Gang, he told himself firmly. Otherwise, he might find himself in a rather great deal of danger.

"Do I look that bad?" Nancy said, glancing at the new silk gown, raising a hand to her hair, which had been inexpertly pinned. "My sister usually helps with my—"

"You look fine," Byron said decisively.

Fine? Fine? He wanted to cry to the rooftops just how exquisite she looked! But that would never do. It would be mortifying indeed to reveal just how instantly he was attracted to her.

A look of disappointment swiftly moved across Nancy's face before being replaced by one of stoic readiness. "Well, are you prepared to leave?"

Byron sighed as he looked at the sofa. Poxy thing. It had looked perfectly comfortable when they had arrived last night, exhausted enough to give this innkeeper the same lie as the previous one.

"Yes, we'd like two rooms—ah. You have one. Well, that will be perfectly suitable for my, uh, wife and me..."

He had volunteered to take the sofa because he was a gentleman, Byron told himself, trying to ignore the flecks of pain still moving up his spine. A duke would never permit a lady to sleep on a sofa!

Except that now he thought about it, she was shorter. Only by a little, but that may have made all the difference on the sofa last night...

"From now on, I will sleep in the coach if there is no second bedchamber," Byron said firmly, rearranging the cushion and groaning as he stepped forward toward his trunk.

Nancy shook her head with a wry smile. "Where do you think Campion is sleeping?"

Byron stared as she moved to the window and opened the curtains. A gray, quiet sort of day was dawning. Little sunlight was making its way through the clouds, and it looked as though it might rain later.

Campion? Where he was...he hadn't even given the matter a second thought.

Why would he? Byron reasoned. His servants always looked

after themselves, didn't they? It was hardly his concern to ensure they had bed and board. They were his servants. They would be accorded the same honorable treatment, as servants of a duke, that they always…

Ah. Only now did it occur to him, as Nancy bustled around him and made the bed—*why, he could not think*—that as he was traveling incognito, Campion probably wasn't being afforded that respectful treatment.

If they had brought the carriage with the ducal livery on, that would be different. The innkeepers may even have been able to find additional bedchambers, Byron thought with a sinking feeling in his chest. They had not known they were speaking to a duke, had they?

Oh, bother.

"He's…he's sleeping in the carriage?"

Nancy turned with such a surprised look on her face, Byron was quite mortified. "Where on earth did you think he was sleeping? The stables?"

Byron did not answer. Discomfort was creeping up his chest in a most disconcerting way. Perhaps if he did not speak, did not make even more of a fool of himself than he already had, it would go away.

"Besides, that's not our greatest concern," said Nancy nonchalantly, stepping to the door.

"And what is that?"

Byron had not considered his question to be particularly radical, but she stopped with her hand on the door and an astonished look.

"You…you really don't know?"

He swallowed. It was never pleasant to feel the fool, and he'd been doing that a lot recently. Snee, having to cancel on his attendance at the Caelfall wedding—he was never going to hear the end of that. And now this.

So what did Nancy Mead know that he didn't?

"What else can there be?" Byron tried to point out, shrugging as nonchalantly as he could manage. "We have a mail coach refusing to take the regular roads, lost somewhere in the Kentish countryside. We have horses getting more tired by the day, dwindling money—"

"And scandal."

Byron blinked. *Scandal?*

Nancy's eyes were dancing with something that on any other woman would have been described as mischief, but it couldn't be. Surely she couldn't be...delighted there was some sort of scandal attached to them?

"I merely meant," she said lightly, "that when I return to London, my reputation will be ruined. I am going to have to give some sort of account as to my absence to my landlady. And my employer. Although, I think after my sudden disappearance, with not so much as a word or a note, they are probably my employer no longer."

Byron stared. *Employer? Landlady? Absence?*

And then it hit him. Of course. He was a duke, able to gallivant about the place, utterly unconcerned with the suspicions of the *ton*. He had their favor. Every duke had, up to a point. It was almost impossible to think of one—save perhaps for Martock—who had seriously displeased society.

He could disappear with his bag of money, and his servants would continue on with their work, keeping his home busy and warm.

But Nancy?

"Your...your landlady," he repeated weakly.

Nancy frowned. "What, did you think I owned my own home?"

Byron felt foolish saying it. "Well, yes."

Did not everyone own their own home? The very idea they would not...

She was laughing, which only made him feel even more of a fool. "Byron, not all of us have pots of money, you know."

"I didn't say—"

"And as a woman, I cannot even earn mine, at least not without losing my respectability," Nancy said ruefully. "There's a reason Lady Romeril no longer comes to call."

Byron stiffened. *Lady Romeril? Dear lord, that meant...*

Well, that if the Mead family fortunes had not become so damaged, however it had happened, then Nancy—Miss Mead would be an intricate part of his own social circle.

To think. Should fate have been different, only ever so slightly, it would have been a very different meeting they would have enjoyed...

And then something else she had said caught up with him.

"Wait—your employer?"

Nancy nodded. "Oh, it's just light work. I am a lady born and bred," she said with a wry smile. "There's not much else I am good for other than copying out sheet music."

Byron stared. She spoke so...so lightly, as though it were commonplace for a lady to be forced to paid employment. As though she had lived with this frustration for many years. Perhaps she had. Perhaps it was now such a part of her life that she found it difficult to consider that it could be any other way.

Most odd.

"What, you are shocked because you have spent the last few days with a woman who gets her hands dirty?"

The phrase jerked Byron from his thoughts. "What do you—"

"Ink can get absolutely everywhere, you know," said Nancy with a teasing smile.

Byron was in real danger. This wasn't just the habitual flirtation of a woman who had spent so much time in good society that she hardly knew what the rest of the world was.

This was a woman who had fought, evidently, to keep her family together. Who had lowered herself to take up paid employment if it could mean keeping her siblings secure. Who was willing to risk everything, anything to bring them to safety.

Byron's chest tightened as his breathing became difficult, looking deep into Nancy's eyes. He would have to be careful here. It would be all too easy to—

Something she had said flickered through her mind. "Your reputation will be ruined?"

Nancy gestured around the small bedchamber then opened the door. "You don't think a lady's reputation is destroyed when it is discovered she has been traveling for several days with a man to whom she is not married?"

Byron's stomach lurched. She was right. There was no one better for knowing the sticking points of society, he had always found, than the ladies.

And guilt, strong and potent, washed over him.

This was his fault. He could have stopped her—well, perhaps not. But he could have put up a great deal more effort to prevent her from joining him on what he was certain Snee was going to call a fool's errand.

Careening around the country desperately in search of a mail coach about to be attacked by the most notorious gang in all England...and he had brought a woman with him?

Well, he knew what the world would think.

If he had heard about it, he would probably have thought the same thing. That the woman was a mere bit of skirt, designed to distract the man on his hunt for the Glasshand Gang when he had a dull moment.

Byron almost snorted as they reached the bottom of the stairs and turned into the dining area, where a few other patrons were breaking their fast.

Dull moment? With Nancy?

"Yes, two for breakfast, please bring it straight over," Nancy was saying to the man Byron vaguely remembered to be the innkeeper. "And tea. Lots of tea."

Byron allowed himself to merely follow Nancy to a table and sit as his mind raced.

He had never thought much of his own reputation. He'd never had to. He was a duke. Reputation was something one inherited, much like the pile in the country and the kitchen staff.

"You look deep in thought," remarked Nancy, beaming at the serving maid who brought over two plates. "Oh, delicious!"

Byron had to admit the food did look good. More toast than he had ever seen before was placed between them in a stack as a platter of butter and jams joined it. On the plates put before them were rashers of bacon, fried eggs, potatoes, mushrooms, tomatoes...

"Just what we need before a day of mail coach hunting," said Nancy with a teasing grin. "Thank you, just the tea left to come, I think..."

Byron tried to concentrate on the food. He knew it would be important to have a good breakfast before they disappeared off to find the mail coach. To find the Glasshand Gang...

"Byron?"

He jerked to attention. "I beg your pardon?"

"Your breakfast is getting cold," Nancy pointed out.

Byron looked down. Her plate was already half empty, and she had managed to make a good indent into the stack of toast. "Ah. Yes. So it is."

Picking up his knife and fork, he commenced eating. And it was delicious, precisely what he needed. And yet...

Byron put down his knife and fork. "Nancy."

She grinned. "Byron."

"This isn't a laughing matter," he said severely, his heart twisting in pain. If she were to lose her reputation, all because he had not been sensible enough to pull her out of his carriage... "You were serious, weren't you?"

Nancy waited, then asked, "About what?"

"About losing your—" Byron caught himself just in time and lowered his voice. Their table was quite close by. "Losing your reputation."

Her smile flickered just for a moment. "It is of no matter."

"It is of great import, and you know that," he said severely. Did the woman purposefully try to be contrary? "It would be disastrous indeed for you to return to London with such rumors flying at your heels."

"Yes, but there is not a great deal I can do about it, is there?"

Byron hesitated. What he was about to suggest was madness. Foolish. If it had been anyone else, he would not even think of it.

But this was Nancy. Though he had only known her a few days, he felt a connection to her deeper than he had ever experienced with anyone else. And those kisses...

"We could pretend...to be married."

Nancy raised an eyebrow. "I thought we already—"

"I mean, when you return, you can say that you were married," Byron said, the words slipping carelessly from his lips. "Married, and widowed."

Nancy's face paled. "You're not suggesting—"

"We don't actually have to be wed, of course, and I fully intend not to die to boot," he said with what he hoped was a wry grin. "It would give you the excuse of where you had been, and the respectability of a widow."

"A working widow," she pointed out.

Their breakfasts between them lay forgotten. Their conversation had slipped into something dark and mysterious, important. Byron could hardly understand it, but no words exchanged had ever borne such weight.

What on earth was he suggesting? And why did this feel...so right?

"We have to save those nine people, and we're not going to get there in time if we constantly have to think of how to pretend on the road," Byron said urgently, his voice still low. "I think this is the best plan. F-For both of us."

And what he didn't say, but thought desperately, was how much he wished to kiss her again. How, if they were pretending to be newlyweds, they may have to kiss. Just once or twice. To prove to landlords, innkeepers, tollbooth men...

Nancy was biting her lip. "How much danger is the mail coach in, Byron?"

Byron stiffened. Memories flooded his mind, of pain, anguish, rushed promises given in the dead of night to a dying man...

"Great danger," he said finally.

Nancy sighed, examining him closely. "Fine."

Byron blinked. "I beg your pard—"

"Pass the jam, husband," she said cheerfully. "We should be on the road in ten minutes."

CHAPTER TWELVE

A LTHOUGH NANCY HAD never traveled on a ship before, this was what she had imagined.

The gentle sway of the carriage. The wind whistling past them, the fabric whipping in the breeze. The way the landscape through the window never seemed to change, yet if you looked away for an hour or so, it was suddenly completely different. The weather had such an impact. Then the constant need to stay still yet the yearning to walk about.

Nancy smiled as her gaze flickered around the carriage. She had thought it rather impressive when she had first helped herself to a seat. And it still was in a way.

The cushioned seats were still there. There was still a blanket on the side to cover her legs when the chilly autumnal air threatened to seep through the cracks into the carriage.

But it was different, somehow.

Smaller, perhaps. Nancy certainly felt as though there was less air in the place. The presence of a handsome man who was doing nothing but infuriating her then making her feel so warm and soft was playing havoc with her ability to concentrate.

But for now, as he slept, she watched him. The way his chest slowly moved, his cravat loose, his top shirt button open. His green coat had been removed and was now placed over him like a blanket—a suggestion he had rolled his eyes at when she had first done it, but he was now curled up underneath it.

Nancy's stomach twisted. It was not an unpleasant feeling, more an unexpected one.

What on earth was she doing?

Byron shifted in his sleep, turning his face to the window, the arch of his jawline even more obvious. She tried not to notice, but it was like pretending the sun was not there, or that rain wasn't wet.

Byron Renwick was a good-looking man, but more than that, he had a good soul. At least, that was what she assumed was driving this determination to catch the Glasshand Gang.

What else could it be?

Nancy had spoken the truth earlier that morning when she had told Byron her reputation was all but gone.

"I merely meant that when I return to London, my reputation will be ruined."

Possible it may be to pretend she had been wed, the very idea of returning as a fake widow to London was not something Nancy could countenance. How could she keep that sort of thing a secret? How could she pretend, for the rest of her life, that she had known the sweet touch of a spouse?

And that was without even thinking how she could attempt to explain to Matthew and Beth…

Nancy smiled despite herself. Well, perhaps on paper this whole escapade was a mistake—but it didn't feel like it.

For the first time in her life, she had spoken with a man who treated her as an equal. A person. Not a woman conniving to catch a man, not a simpering miss who didn't have two thoughts in her head.

This felt right. And though she knew the deception was false, it almost felt like—

"Where are we?"

Nancy started. She had grown so lost in her thoughts, she had not noticed Byron's sleepy eyes open.

She shrugged. "I am not entirely sure. Your driver muttered something about—"

"Oh, well, if he thinks he knows what he is doing, far be it from me to attempt to dissuade him," said Byron heavily, sitting more upright.

Nancy examined him with curiosity. "You have an odd relationship with your servants, don't you?"

She had not intended her words to be quite so direct, but then, that was the sort of person she was. There was no point attempting to change her character, not now.

Besides, Byron did not seem particularly offended. He looked intrigued. "What makes you say that?"

"Well, most people would query their servants a little more, wish to ascertain they were doing what was expected," said Nancy, trying to find words to explain the feeling deep within her. "You...trust him."

"Trust Campion? Of course I do," said Byron with a grin. "He served my father, and his father served my—"

"Goodness!" Nancy stared, wide-eyed. "Truly?"

What an unusual situation. Everyone wished to find the servant who would stay with a family, working hard for many years. A decade or more was something to be hoped for, but rarely seen.

But the idea of a person doing that, and their father or mother performing the exact same job for the same family...

"I have only ever heard of that sort of thing happening with the very best of families," she said as the carriage rattled along.

Byron raised an eyebrow. "Dear me. Are you saying that you presumed my family was not of the very best?"

There was such an arch, teasing tone in his voice that Nancy allowed herself to relax. "What, you think yourself as fine as an earl perhaps, or a marquess?"

For a moment, just a moment—but no, it must have been a trick of the light. It was hard to tell within a carriage moving so quickly. Just a flicker across Byron's face. It could have been amusement. Whatever it was, the emotion had gone before she'd had a chance to fully understand it.

Byron grinned. "Could you imagine? Me, an earl?"

The thought was ridiculous. A warm sort of playfulness rose in Nancy's heart—something she rarely had the opportunity to feel.

When one was attempting to keep together a family that had essentially fallen apart, levity was a luxury, not a part of everyday life.

"I would have to call you 'my lord,' I suppose," she said with a quirk of her lips.

Byron chuckled. "Goodness, it would be strange to hear myself called that."

"And I do not suppose an earl would have permitted himself to fall asleep before me," Nancy added, her heart leaping in the pleasure of the game. "And…"

Her voice trailed away. She had made a mistake; how, she was not sure, but all the joy had disappeared from Byron's face and he now looked distinctly uncomfortable.

"I suppose that was rather a liberty," he said stiffly. "My apologies."

Nancy stared. What sort of a man apologized for falling asleep? He was no earl, but evidently Byron had been raised in a stilted way. His family had money, and from the little she knew of society, there was nothing worse in some quarters than having plenty of money but none of the respect a title would bring.

That must have been how Byron had been raised. Poor man. No wonder he was so…so uncomfortable so much of the time.

"Please do not concern yourself," she said quietly. "It is hardly your fault that you are sleeping so ill at the moment."

He looked up sharply at her words. "What do you mean?"

It appeared so obvious to Nancy, she felt odd saying it aloud. "Well, the last two nights we have attempted to find accommodation at inns. On both occasions, you have suffered the sofa rather than a bed."

She watched as Byron relaxed, his shoulders lowering, some of the worry unfurling from his brow.

What had he thought she meant?

"Oh, I see," he said softly. His gaze flickered to the window. "Well, it is not your fault. Much."

"You think I should have given up the bed for you?" Nancy said hesitantly. *Was that too teasing?* Would she ever learn precisely where the lines were for this man between laughter and pain?

"Oh no, I did not mean it like that," Byron said with haste, turning back to her. "It's more...well. I have never slept well since..."

And then he appeared to have second thoughts.

Nancy watched him closely. She had thought he had a secret, something he was holding back, from the moment she had met him. The days which had past had not disabused her of that notion.

The real reason he was chasing after the Glasshand Gang...

It could not be merely because there was someone in that mail coach. He had spoken of no one. She'd been hard pressed to stop herself talking about her sister throughout their journey the moment she had admitted to her existence.

Whether Beth was warm, whether she had any idea the Glasshand Gang was coming for them, what she would do once they caught up with the coach...

But Byron had said nothing of this person he was apparently attempting to save.

"My wife. I mean my sister!"

Nancy frowned. There was no wife, sister, or friend, she was sure. Byron was an open book in many ways; he would have spoken of her. Yet he remained silent.

So what was his purpose in chasing after the Glasshand Gang? What spurred him on?

And just how far would he go to catch them?

"You know, Byron," Nancy said quietly. "I feel as though I

know you so well in many ways."

His gaze met hers and the silent response was so loud, she flushed. Yes, their kissing was not to be repeated. If she could feel like all this from just one look, she was in far more danger than she had initially thought.

"But at the same time, I know very little of you," she persisted, forcing herself to continue speaking. "You know so much about me, my family, my troubles."

Byron's lips twisted into a wry smile. "And you think I should share the same?"

"I would not demand confidences," she said hastily. "It's more...well. If you would like to share anything. It is not as though there is any other sort of distraction."

She gestured around the carriage. Her point was plain.

Nancy waited, watching Byron carefully as he remained silent. She could almost see his mind whirring, like a clock's mechanism. What was he afraid of? What did he think she should not hear? What did he believe would disgrace him in her eyes if he should reveal it?

And then he spoke. His words were so unexpected, Nancy's breath caught in her throat.

"What is it that plagues you in those nightmares?"

Nancy tried to control her thoughts, tried to push all fear from her mind, but it was impossible. Matthew, screaming her name. Beth, lost and distressed, crying out for aid but alone. Herself, trying desperately to reach them, unable to find them in the growing dark—

"Why do you ask?" she said, hoping her words would force memories away.

Byron did not cease his gaze. "What are they about, Nancy?"

Nancy swallowed. She had never spoken of the nightmares, not to anyone. They had started years ago, such a part of her life she did not expect anything different when she laid her head on a pillow.

To sleep without them...it was a fantasy, something she

could never attain.

But speaking them out loud, that would give them power over her, wouldn't it? Allow them to reclaim her waking, as well as her sleeping, life.

Or would it be the opposite? Would Byron help her chase the nightmares away?

"I..." Nancy swallowed. Her voice was weak, barely audible over the growing wind.

But he merely sat there, waiting with a patience she had never expected of anyone, let alone a gentleman. But then, Byron was not anything like the idea she had of a gentleman.

"I dream about losing...losing the people I love," Nancy whispered.

For a moment, it was all too much. The fear returned, coursing through her, replacing her blood with nothing but terror. She looked away from Byron, her gaze flickering to the window, but there was nothing there to console her.

She looked back at him and almost gasped.

There was such kindness, such understanding—compassion she had never seen before.

"I understand," Byron said quietly.

Nancy half laughed, her voice choked. "No, you don't. Until you're responsible for the life, for the safety of another, you cannot possibly know! The panic, the fear that never leaves you the moment they are out of your sight—"

"Nancy, I am telling you I understand—"

"And even when they're grown, you can't stop wondering whether they are safe, warm, dry, fed," she continued, her tongue flying out of her control as the words poured out of her. "You think every moment—"

"Nancy, I have the same nightmare."

Nancy halted. Her throat was hoarse, her lungs tight, but as she looked at Byron, all that tension melted away.

He really did understand. It wasn't compassion or pity after all. It was true empathy.

"My father, he…" Byron swallowed, licking his lips as though in a desperate way to find his voice. "He died."

Nancy nodded, but did not speak. There was more to this tale, but she knew better than anyone how hard it was to continue if someone interrupted. Byron needed to tell this story, but in his own time.

It was perhaps a full minute before he spoke again. There was such pained, forced jollity in his voice that Nancy wished she were brave enough to reach out and take his hand.

"I know most people decry their fathers, but mine was rather wonderful. I admired him greatly, respected him. Loved him, I suppose. I never told him that. People in my family never talked about their feelings."

Nancy swallowed. The agony in Byron's voice was palpable.

Byron tried to smile. "Our house, it was being burgled—our steward was attacked; we could hear it outside, and my father—"

She closed her eyes, just for a moment. The carriage rocked, like the ship she had imagined, but this was no sea voyage. This was real life.

She did not need to hear the rest of the tale. She knew what happened, and by who.

"He rushed out and confronted them," Byron said with a heavy sigh and a shake of his head. "I told him I would go. I was younger, fitter. He didn't even wait, just…"

Nancy spoke quietly. "It wasn't your fault, Byron."

"I should have stopped him, I should have faced them myself," he said fiercely. "By the time I got out there, I found him, lying in a—a pool of…and I should have done something!"

There was such raw agony in his words that Nancy felt her throat choke up. *He does understand.*

"The Glasshand Gang," she said softly.

Byron nodded. "Since then, I have—I promised my father, I would repay…they deserve justice."

Nancy forced herself to let out the breath she was holding as her shoulders shuddered.

She had wondered precisely why Byron was seeking the Glasshand Gang—and now she knew. There was no greater force than the desire for justice by a man who had been injured. There were probably few people in the world who had been so wronged by the Glasshand Gang. Who knew their viciousness. Their lack of respect for human life.

And her heart went cold.

Beth is on that mail coach.

"I did not think it possible to respect you more," Nancy murmured.

Byron laughed darkly as he shook his head. "Oh, I don't think it's a particularly noble thing to feel like this. To be eaten up by the hunger for retribution—"

"I would call it justice."

"You can call it whatever you want," said Byron, his words taking on a harsh tone. "My apologies, I did not mean—"

"It's quite alright," said Nancy.

In this moment, she understood why his rage spilled over. If she had found Matthew in such a situation…well, she would not be staying overnight at inns. She would be walking across the wild moors of Kent to find them.

"But you are a gentleman," she could not help but say. "Are you not?"

Byron's head snapped up. "What does that mean?"

Nancy tried to smile as her stomach swooped. "I just…you could pay people to do this, you know. You do not have to be out here yourself, chasing after them. You could—"

"I made a vow to my father, and I have no intention of breaking it," he said with an air of finality. "And you have to do what's right. Even if it is hard."

Nancy nodded. He was right. Or, at least, the fact was so true to him that there was nothing she could offer that would dissuade him from his beliefs.

Now she understood. This was not merely a mission Byron Renwick had been sent to complete on behalf of London justice.

Perhaps it was, but it was also about family, love, and loyalty.

All things she greatly understood.

Nancy fought back the instinct to slip onto his lap and kiss away his fears. *That would do no good*, she told herself. Byron did not need platitudes; he needed justice. Though his kisses would be sweet, it would only further complicate the already complicated feelings she had.

Feelings she should be attempting to avoid.

Still, her body craved his touch in a way she could not articulate. Despite herself, Nancy leaned forward, her fingers entwining with his.

"Byron," she said quietly.

Byron looked up and opened his mouth as though to say something—but no words came out. Instead, only a yawn emerged.

"I am so sorry," he said swiftly as Nancy giggled. "I did not mean to—"

"I know," she said with a dry laugh. "And I am not offended—but I do think you need a little more sleep. Go on."

Byron looked confused. "You...you are happy for me to—"

"You need sleep, man, and that's an order," Nancy said with a mock severity that made him roll his eyes. "Go on. I'll keep an eye out for the mail coach. Don't you fear, I'll call out as soon as we see it."

He did not seem to have enough energy to argue. Pulling his coat toward him as a pillow once more, it was not long before his breathing had slowed, and he had once again fallen into slumber.

Nancy watched him. A protectiveness had sprung up in her that she had never known before. Something more than what she felt for her siblings. Something that demanded she care for him, but at the same time, allow herself to be cared for by him.

It was all rather confusing. Nancy allowed the feelings to billow up before pushing them firmly down. She couldn't permit any of that nonsense.

CHAPTER THIRTEEN

"AND THEN I started talking about the picnic we had taken together in Hyde Park, and she looked at me as though I was spouting gibberish!"

Byron watched, fascinated, as Nancy came alive as she told her story.

She was absolute perfection.

He had never had such a thought about a woman before. About anyone, when it came to that—but then, Byron had not been paying much attention to people for the last year or so.

When one had a vow to make that involved the death of a parent through violence, one had little time for socializing.

"Honestly, I tried to explain, but the more I repeated the tale of the picnic, the more confused she looked..."

Yet here, together, Byron was conscious he was having something he had not experienced for a very long while.

A good time.

The inn they had found was pleasant, far more impressive than the others. The weather had forced them off the road, as it had undoubtedly done to the mail coach. He was trying to accept the further delay with good grace, and the room helped. It was a large private room into which they had been ushered—Byron's hefty two half-crowns had seen to that—and the fire was blazing merrily in the grate.

The bedchamber they had been shown upstairs was also adequate. Byron had worked hard to keep his face calm as he had heard the predicament.

"Only one bedchamber, you say?" he had said, as nonchalantly as he could manage. "Well, fancy that."

"I do not know why you are so concerned, husband dear," Nancy had said with a flicker of mischief in her eyes. "Are you saying you wish to be apart from me?"

Oh, Byron could have fallen to the floor at such a statement. Thankfully, the innkeeper did not seem to have noticed just how red his cheeks must have become at such a statement. *Thankfully.* It would do for the world to think he was actually enamored with his wife.

With Nancy. Goodness, that was a mistake not to be repeated aloud.

"—I even tried to remind her just what Lady Romeril had said at the picnic, but Miss Lymington was having absolutely none of it!" Nancy said with a laugh, pausing to take a sip of wine. "Well, you could imagine what I was thinking."

Byron leaned forward on his elbows, absolutely captivated. "Go on."

Nancy's eyes twinkled. "Well…"

He had never met anyone who could tell a story like Nancy. Byron had been entertained by her all afternoon, after his second and most refreshing nap. She had a sharp yet kind way of looking at the world, which made her an excellent travel companion.

Indeed, Byron could think of no one else he would rather have been traveling with. She was an absolute delight. Perhaps too delightful.

He shifted uncomfortably in the rich leather seat by the table. With the candlelight and flickering firelight, Nancy's hair was a wash of fiery flames. Her eyes glittered; the moisture of her lips glistened.

And whenever she leaned forward to tell him a particularly

juicy part of the tale, or to take in a mouthful of particularly delicious food, there was a curve to her breasts Byron could not help but notice.

Well, he was hardly a monk! A man had desires, didn't he?

Byron swallowed. At least, he had always had them and never permitted himself to...

"And then of course," Nancy said with a tinkling laugh. "I remembered."

He leaned forward. "Remembered?"

"Miss Lymington is not an only child."

He frowned. "So, she had a sister."

"Almost," said Nancy with another giggle. "She has a twin sister!"

Byron could not help but laugh. "No—no, there is absolutely no way that you—"

"I promise, it is the complete truth," said Nancy firmly, shaking her head at the mere memory of her story. "There I was, sitting at a table with what I thought was Miss Olivia Lymington, and instead, I had spent the last half an hour conversing with her identical twin!"

They laughed, their joy rolling around the room and filling the place with such a warm atmosphere. Byron was hit by a strange thought. *We never have to leave this place.*

The idea was fleeting. They had to find the mail coach. The only reason he had agreed to stop off this night was because of two threats.

Firstly, Campion had been adamant another storm was coming in, an even larger one than a few nights ago. Rolling straight off the coast, he had said. Danger to life and property. There had been nothing for it, at least in Byron's eyes, than stopping at the nearest available inn.

And secondly, Nancy had threatened that if she did not stop off for a good meal, she would overturn the carriage.

"Well, I'm hungry," she had said defensively as Byron had rolled his eyes at the time. "A woman needs something more than a good breakfast to keep going!"

And so, with the inevitability of a man who knew there was absolutely no point in attempting to argue with her, Byron had given the order to stop at the next inn. Thankfully, it was impressive, and so was the dinner.

It was the conversation, however, that really sparkled.

"And the whole time, she had said nothing to me," continued Nancy. "I was made to feel a complete fool."

"What did you say to her the next time you saw her?" Byron inquired.

It was fascinating to hear the tale. Mistaken identity and identical twins were not something one heard about every day, after all, but it was more than that. The way Nancy told a story involving her whole body, her face beautiful yet expressive, the way she could draw him into a tale...

Byron swallowed. *As though nothing else mattered.*

"Well, in fact, I never did," said Nancy with a wry shake of her head.

He waited for the rest of the explanation, but for some reason, it didn't come. He watched her pick at the remainder of her food, all the joy somehow seeping out of the room.

Had he said something wrong? Had he presumed something he should not have? Byron swallowed, an unfamiliar feeling of disquiet settling in his stomach.

He was the Duke of Sedley. Being a part of a joyful conversation was par for the course, but usually, the conversation happened around him. Toward him. The contributions he made were usually his presence only. After all, who did not want to enjoy dinner with a duke?

But this was different. Nancy was not impressed by his title— *only because she does not know it,* Byron could not help but think.

In a way, he regretted that. If he had told her, would she already have invited him into her bed?

Byron allowed the thought to linger for a moment before he ignored it. No, he could not think like that. It would be most unfair of him to presume upon Nancy's heart—or her body. Even if he wished to.

And in a way, it was pleasant, sitting with a person who did not know they should address him as "Your Grace". Freeing in a way he had never known before.

"Why didn't you?" he prompted, eager to hear the rest of the story.

Nancy glanced up, a knowing look through her eyelashes. "My father's fortune was lost just the week after. For some reason, most of our invitations dried up. It simply was not possible for anyone to permit our company."

Byron's stomach curled. *The Cut.* Well, it happened—though usually for a far more important reason than the lack of a fortune.

But that was the way society worked, as he well knew. Did not his family uphold many of the fine traditions? And would he decide that a woman with charm but few prospects was no longer a suitable dinner companion?

It would have been obvious...before he met Nancy.

"I am sorry," he found himself saying.

Nancy sipped her wine. "Do not trouble yourself; it was not your fault."

"But still—"

"If you had any sway over the *ton*, of course, that would be different," she teased, her playful air returning as her hair shimmered under the candlelight. "But you don't."

Byron swallowed. *Well...*

No. There was nothing to be gained by revealing his true identity now. He had already revealed far too much of himself already—parts of himself he had never shared with another.

Telling the story of his father's demise was something that had never escaped the rest of the family. Not that he had promised to keep it a secret, but it had been painful. Too painful to share.

Until Nancy.

"Anyway, if you thought my mistake with the Lymington

twins was bad, you should hear about the time I accidentally forgot to let Lady Romeril win at cards," teased Nancy.

Byron's mouth fell open. "You didn't!"

"You know her then?"

"I do not believe there is a person alive who does not know Lady Romeril," said Byron without thinking. Then he added, "Or at the very least, know of her."

She was, after all, a formidable woman. She had once informed Byron, quite calmly, that his father had proposed matrimony to her, but she had declined him because she was afraid that he would lose his hair as he aged.

He had informed her, quite boldly, that his father had not lost his hair.

And she had replied, with an arched brow, "And that, my dear, is because he was not married to me."

"Lady Romeril is fearsome indeed," Byron said aloud, with some feeling. "Especially when she plays at cards."

"I know—or at least, I know now," said Nancy with a laugh. "But the trouble was…"

Byron relaxed as Nancy settled into another amusing tale. Truly, he could sit here for hours if given the privilege of listening to her. There was something about the way she could craft a tale, as though she was well aware of how precisely her audience liked to be amused.

As though she knows me, Byron could not help but think.

Perhaps she did. He had been far more open and vulnerable with her than anyone. There was little she did not know of him. Just one or two things…

"You're smiling."

Byron started. "I beg your pardon?"

Her tale forgotten, Nancy laid down her knife and fork. "Oh, you were listening, but only in that polite way gentlemen have when their minds are elsewhere."

His stomach turned. "I wasn't—"

"You don't have to lie to me, you know," she said softly.

"You never have to. You can just be honest. Be yourself."

Byron swallowed.

"You don't have to lie to me, you know. You never have to. You can just be honest. Be yourself."

Those words had never been spoken to him before—and they had never been demonstrated either. Being a duke, being someone who had responsibilities...the assumption was that he would always be the duke. Always be the Duke of Sedley.

Being Byron Renwick on this adventure had been like nothing else, but he had not realized that until now. Until he looked into Nancy's eyes and saw her warm acceptance.

"You are such good company, Nancy," Byron said quietly. "I could almost forget the reason that we are here."

Her smile was warm, unaffected. "You know, although this entire adventure, or whatever you want to call it, is dangerous, and our loved ones are in peril, I have rather enjoyed myself. Even if it is to end tomorrow."

Byron's stomach dropped.

End tomorrow?

"Campion says that there is such little distance now between Dover and ourselves, it is inevitable we will run into the mail coach," Nancy continued, utterly unaware of what he had just felt. "And I will see my sister again, and you will find..." Her voice trailed off delicately.

Byron tried to smile. *Ah, yes.* His pathetic lie. He wished he had never said anything so foolish.

"My wife. I mean my sister!"

How on earth was he supposed to explain he had no person on that mail coach to save? That his heart was full of nothing but a desire for revenge?

Well. Perhaps another desire too...

"I will miss you," Byron said quietly.

The words were entirely unintentional, but they were true. There was something about Nancy's presence that brought peace to his heart. A peace he had been seeking in the downfall of the

Glasshand Gang, but apparently could be found here, too. If only he looked hard enough.

He had not even been looking. Yet here she was.

"Byron," Nancy said awkwardly. "I—"

"Anything else you need, sir, m'lady?" said a maid loudly as she stepped into the room.

Byron gripped the stem of his wine glass at his frustration. *She had been about to say something—something important!*

"Nothing, I thank you," he snapped. "Please leave us and ensure no one disturbs."

The serving maid bobbed a curtsey and shot them both a curious look before departing.

Byron turned immediately back to Nancy. "You were saying?"

"I was?"

The temptation to curse under his breath was strong, but he managed to avoid it. "You said my name, and then I thought…it was as though you were going to say something important."

Yes, there was definitely something unexpected in those eyes of hers. Nerves. What could she be nervous about?

Unless, Byron thought, heart racing, she was about to tell him something important. Unless there was something more to reveal about the mail coach—or she was secretly a part of the Glasshand Gang—or she was in love with him—

"I honestly cannot think what it could have been," said Nancy, not quite meeting his gaze. "I am sure if it was important, it will come back to me."

Byron hesitated, but though he wished to do something, how did one encourage another to reveal feelings? If she felt anything for him at all, that was. He was hardly certain what he felt for her.

"More wine?" Byron said. "Here, I'll take your—"

"Let me pass you my—"

He gasped. So did Nancy, or at least, that was what he thought he heard. He could hardly tell, thanks to the ringing in his ears.

In that moment, they had both reached for her wine glass, her to pass it to him, him to bring it to the bottle neck of the wine.

The same thought at the same time.

Their fingers had touched and sparks had flown through Byron, sparks so hot he was scalded. Scalded by a tension between them which had been bubbling under the surface, now coming to the fore in a wash of tempting, promising pleasure.

"Oh, I do apologize," said Byron, moving to pull back his hand.

But he could not. Nancy's fingers had somehow become entangled with his own. There was no way of returning his hand to his lap, short of wrenching it away.

And that, he had no desire to do.

"Byron," whispered Nancy, staring at their entwined fingers.

Byron's heart was roaring so fast he could barely hear the individual beats. He knew what he wanted, what any man would want, faced with beauty and wit such as Nancy had.

But he would be no cad of that degree. He knew the sort of man who would take advantage of a woman in that manner, and he was never going to be that man. Not like—

"Nancy," he breathed, unable to help himself.

Oh, this was heavenly. The sense of her skin brushing up against his, the pulse he could feel—was that hers, or his own? It did not matter. Perhaps their heart beat as one in this heady moment that promised so much yet could offer so little.

Even if he wanted more. So, so much more.

"N-Nancy, I know there is only one bed up there," Byron said, voice faltering. "And I know you are a lady, and would have no wish to—"

"I am happy for you to be in the bed," Nancy said breathlessly.

It was all Byron could do not to fall off his chair. *She was happy, instantly willing to accept his request?*

"Y-You are?"

"Oh, yes, I am sure there will be a sofa in there that will be sufficient for me."

And Byron's heart sank. *Of course, that was the most decorous approach.* There could be no other alternative. He was the one with such forbidden desires, not her.

"Ah," he said helplessly.

Nancy swallowed, her fingers twisting in his own. "Unless…"

"Unless?"

"Unless you were thinking of something else," she said, her voice barely above a breath. "Something more."

And Byron knew this was it. Now or never. As he looked into her eyes, unable to take in all her beauty for it was so splendid, he knew he had to ask.

Ask, or die regretting it.

"Nancy, I am—I have become very fond of you."

Something died in her eyes. "Fond?"

Byron cursed his own ineptitude. If he had ever done this before, he would at least know what he was doing!

He had been astonished she was able to wheedle out of him the story of his father. He held two other great secrets, secrets he'd promised to keep to himself. Perhaps this was the moment for another one to be revealed.

"Nancy, I have never loved a woman before. Never bedded one, never held one, never…never kissed one before. Not until you." Byron held his breath.

Nancy's mouth fell open. "You—you cannot be in earnest!"

"I know it probably makes me unusual in the world of men, but it is the truth," Byron said ruefully, wishing to goodness he felt bolder. "I have never—it was not for lack of wanting, but…well. I never met a woman I felt would be truly worth the intimacy. Until you."

Until I saw you, he wanted to say. *Until I grew to know you: your bravery, your heart, your determination. Beauty you have, yes, but there's so much more.*

Perhaps one day, he would be able to tell her. In this moment, however, Byron felt his heart once again sink as Nancy pulled her hand away.

So. His affection was not reciprocated. He was merely an entertainment on the road. He should have known.

"Well," she said, glancing up with pink cheeks. "What a thing to say to your wife."

"If only," Byron said before he could stop himself.

And now Nancy truly did meet his eyes. "If only what?"

CHAPTER FOURTEEN

"W ELL. WHAT A *thing to say to your wife.*"
"*If only.*"
"*If only what?*"

Nancy would have swallowed, but there did not appear to be sufficient moisture in her mouth.

She had said it now. It was not the sort of sentence one could unsay.

The trouble was, it did not appear that Byron had heard her. There was no movement in his face, no twitch in his mouth, no dawn of understanding in his eyes. If his chest had not been moving, she would have assumed there was something direly wrong.

But there he sat, simply staring, as though he had never seen a woman before.

Perhaps he hadn't. Not really seen one.

Nancy could not stop thinking about the words that he had said mere minutes ago…

"*I have never—it was not for lack of wanting, but…well. I never met a woman I felt would be truly worth the intimacy. Until you.*"

He could not mean what she thought he meant…could he? It seemed so unlikely, so preposterous. Here was a man who was handsome, charming—infuriating at times, but wealthy. Most ladies would happily accept the attentions of such a man. Many women, Nancy was sure, would allow their virtue to be taken.

The idea she was not merely one of a small number of women who had heartily kissed Byron Renwick, but the only one? The first?

It was a heady thought.

But she could not dwell on that now. Byron swallowed, and in that instant, Nancy saw the emotion in his eyes.

Hunger.

Not for food. They had been well cared for here at this inn; there could be no complaints about the fare that had been brought to their table.

No, this was an entirely different sort of hunger. One, she hoped, only she could satisfy.

"Byron?" Nancy said uncertainly.

She was not sure what she had expected, but it wasn't this. In her imagination—something she rarely permitted to explore—she had thought such an invitation, veiled as it was, would have encouraged a response.

Any response.

But Byron still continued to sit there. As though he could barely understand her.

Perhaps, Nancy thought wildly, she had spoken in too low a voice.

And then Byron spoke, quietly and with no malice. "That's the wine talking."

Fury sparked in Nancy's heart. How did he manage that? Always ready to annoy her just as she had decided she truly cared about him!

"It is not," she said firmly, rather undoing the certainty in her tones by knocking her hand against her plate as she spoke.

The rattle of the cutlery seemed to bring Byron to his senses. "You cannot understand what you are asking—"

"I absolutely do," Nancy breathed, knowing the emotion that had stirred in her heart and was now filling every inch of her was nothing but love.

Love. She loved him. Byron.

For his passion, yes, but for his honor. His nobility. The way he cared so deeply about a family member who was gone. They shared the same values, the same desire for excitement, otherwise they would not have found themselves on this journey.

So why not share everything else? Why not give into the cravings they had fought ever since they had both entered his carriage?

Nancy swallowed. *She wanted him.*

"I know you feel it too," she said quietly.

Byron dropped his gaze, but it returned almost in an instant. "You...I..."

Nancy waited. She had to give him time, she knew. If he was truly as innocent as she was, then what she was asking him was far more important than a mere delightful tumble.

No, it was sharing something far more intimate.

Excitement flickered across her skin as anticipation whispered sweet promises. Promises that could only be fulfilled if Byron...

He hesitated, his dark eyes flashing with desire and longing, but also fear. "It would not be fair of me to ask you for...for that."

"You didn't," Nancy pointed out softly.

Byron breathed a shaky laugh. "You know what I mean!"

"What, that I am under your protection?"

"You say that like it is a joke," he said with a growl.

Nancy tried to calm her breathing. Never before did she think she would be in this position—that of encouraging a man to take her to his bed.

But Byron was not like other men. He had far higher values, more honor than he knew what to do with. And he would not permit himself to do something he felt was wrong.

The trouble was, that only made her admire him all the more.

"You can bluff all you want," Nancy whispered, eyes not leaving his. "But I want you, Byron. I want to feel your kisses again, feel the touch of your hand—"

Byron groaned, dropping his head into his hands. "Christ's sake, Nancy!"

"And I know you want it too," she persisted, pushing past embarrassment in the hope of finding something true. "Byron, tell me you don't want me."

He looked up through splayed fingers with desperation. "You know I cannot do that."

The dark throb of his voice sent a shiver up Nancy's smile. "Well then." She rose, napkin falling to the floor. She did not look down, but instead extended a hand. "Just one night," she whispered. "One night to share everything. All we are. All we want."

Nancy watched him swallow, saw the struggle in his face, but knew he would succumb. Knew he wanted her, perhaps far more than she wanted him.

Byron's chair fell back to the floor as he suddenly rose. "Nancy Mead, you temptress."

She smiled wistfully at his eager tone as he took her hand. "Something like that."

It was fortunate indeed that the innkeeper had pointed out their room before they had entered their private parlor, for Nancy's mind was whirling frantically. As they stepped out into the main dining hall, she tried not to meet anyone's gaze. They would guess. Somehow, they would know.

They will only see a pair of newlyweds, Nancy tried to tell herself, carefully tucking her hand behind Byron's so they would not see the absence of a ring. That was all.

The gossip from this Kentish inn would not follow them back to London after…after she and Byron departed.

And the thought of leaving him, no longer spending all day and all night in his company, cut into Nancy's heart like a knife. Her grip on his hand tightened. She would have him.

They had almost made it to their bedchamber before a man appeared in the corridor, beaming.

"Ah, the newlyweds," he said cheerfully. "Off to bed, eh?"

Nancy flushed. The man meant well—he was the innkeeper, but the last thing she needed was innuendo.

"Go away, man, and leave us in peace," Byron said stiffly, pulling her forward.

Her cheeks were scarlet, burning with unexpected surprise as Byron shut the door behind them. The bedchamber they were standing in was perhaps the most impressive they had found on their travels.

The four-poster bed was wide, more than enough for two. A copious number of pillows and blankets covered it, and a fire was ablaze in the fireplace. The curtains were lush velvet, obscuring the windows, and there were a number of pleasing rugs on the floor.

None of which Nancy could take in. She was far more interested in the man standing beside her.

"Well, here we are," said Byron helplessly. "What do we—Nancy!"

All he could manage to splutter was her name, for she made it impossible for him to say anything else.

She could hold back no longer. Why should she? She knew what she wanted—who she wanted—and there was nothing now to stop her.

Nancy's lips met Byron's, and both parted, their tongues meeting in a fiery twist of pleasure and desperation.

She whimpered, she could not help it. The force of his body against hers, the heat of his kisses. Parts of her were awakening, parts she had never known before.

How had she lived without this? Without this sense of closeness, of intimacy that could only be found with a person you trusted beyond all measure?

As he kissed her most passionately, reverence transforming slowly into eager hunger, Byron's hands were not loitering. They moved to her waist at first, clutching her to him as though Nancy would disappear if he let go. Then they shifted slowly down until Nancy gasped in his mouth.

Byron broke the kiss. "What?"

Nancy's cheeks must have been red, she was sure they were, for she could feel the heat in them. "It's nothing, it's just—"

"I don't have to touch your buttocks if you—I'm sorry," he said hastily, removing them at once. "I didn't know—"

"Byron Renwick, you place your hands on my buttocks again right this instant."

He stared, as though she had just demanded he take his own head off and hand it to her. "I...I beg your pardon?"

Nancy swallowed. She had not intended to be so direct, of course, but it was what she wanted. Couldn't she ask for what she wanted?

And it was not as though Byron had been with any other lady, knew what a woman wanted. Nancy was only learning, minute to minute, what it was *she* wanted.

"I said, put your hands back where they were," she said softly, trying to smile. "We are both learning, aren't we? I don't know what I am doing any more than you, I think. But it felt nice, having your hands there. I want them back."

She watched as his Adam's apple bobbed, saw the indecision in him—and knew what she had to do.

Nancy reached out and took Byron's hands in her own. Then she moved them, slowly, without breaking eye contact, until they were once again cupping her buttocks.

She allowed a small moan to escape her lips and Byron's eyes darkened. He had to know, had to see what effect this touch was having on her, did he not? Nancy leaned forward in his arms, pressing her breasts against his chest, and felt as well as heard a slow groan emit from his lips.

"God, that feels good," Byron breathed.

"All of you feels good," Nancy said, hardly knowing where these words were coming from, but knowing they were true. "Now, kiss me."

"Nancy—"

"Kiss me, Byron!"

She did not know what came over her—but she certainly knew what came over Byron. His eyes flashed with a craving she had never seen before. Well, she had, but nothing like that intensity.

Byron crushed his lips on hers and pleasure roared through Nancy's chest at the force, the passion, the pent-up furious desire that he had evidently been holding back for so long. Oh, it felt glorious to be so desired! To see the reaction in him that the sensations of her body gave.

"Oh, Nancy," he moaned.

"Byron," Nancy responded eagerly. "I—Byron!"

For some reason, the man had dropped to his knees.

Nancy's eyes widened. Oh, goodness. He wasn't about to...was he?

"Byron," she repeated, putting out a hand as though to halt him in his tracks. This wasn't how—she didn't want him to feel obliged to—

"Nancy, you have to promise me that I am not taking advantage of you."

Nancy blinked. Him, taking advantage of her?

If anyone had asked—not that she would have been able to bear it if someone discovered them like this—she would have said it was the opposite. She was the one who had persuaded him into this. She was the one almost begging Byron to take her.

And he was worried that he was taking advantage of her?

"We both want this," Nancy managed to say through her whirling thoughts. "We...we do, don't we?"

"Very much," breathed Byron. "But you are my first, Nancy. And I...I don't really know what I'm doing."

Nancy's heart softened. It was rare for a gentleman to be this honest, she had to assume. She could not recall anyone in her acquaintance speaking of a man who even considered being this vulnerable.

Goodness, she loved him. Even if she tried not to, she would love him.

"It would only be wrong if I said to stop," Nancy said as Byron remained kneeling on the floor. "And I want you to keep kissing me."

"Oh, I will," said Byron, moving forward on his knees. "But move back a bit, will you?"

Nancy frowned. Move away? Wouldn't that defeat the point?

Still, she did as he had asked. Within three steps, her back hit the wall behind her. Byron moved forward, still on his knees, a gleam of something wicked in his eyes.

"I have always wanted to do this," he breathed. "But until I met you, I didn't know anyone I truly desired enough to...will you trust me?"

"Yes."

Byron blinked. "But you didn't even know what—"

"I trust you, Byron," Nancy said simply, her heart skipping a beat.

It wasn't exactly "I love you", but in a way, it was more special than that. After all, she loved her siblings, but couldn't trust them as far as she could throw them.

But Byron was different. Byron was a man who could be trusted to the ends of the earth. No matter what he wanted to—

"Byron!" Nancy gasped.

Well, it was most shocking. In a sudden movement she could not have predicted, Byron had moved forward again, still on his knees—and lifted her skirts. Before Nancy could say any more, he had slipped under them, his head and shoulders now entirely obscured by her gown.

"Byron?"

He said nothing, but she could feel him. *Oh, goodness, she could feel him.*

Byron's hands touched her inner thighs, just gently, and Nancy quivered. Now she could see why he had asked her to move backward; the wall was providing her with the support that her legs no longer could.

Slowly, he encouraged her feet to move slightly outward,

parting her legs. Nancy's pulse throbbed in her ears. He couldn't be about to…could he?

"Byron!" Nancy whimpered, her hands clutching at the wall for support.

He had kissed her. Not on her inner thigh, but in her secret place.

And the sensation was unparalleled. Nothing could match it: a sudden swoop of decadence, a hint of pleasure, a rush of anticipation—and then his lips were gone.

"Nancy…"

"Byron," Nancy sobbed as he kissed her again.

This time, his tongue lingered, and her knees trembled. He had longed to do this? What pleasure could it possibly bring him to—

"Oh…oh yes," she moaned.

Her eyelashes fluttered closed as Byron's lips met her secret place again, and this time, he did not remove them. His tongue teased along her edge, darted into her, then again, and this time deeper, longer…faster.

Try as she might, it was impossible for Nancy to keep her eyes open. All she could do was marvel at the intensity of his tongue's rhythm, the way it beat out a pulse of pleasure in her very core that was building, building to something she could not imagine but desperately wanted.

And just as she thought she could not take any more—

"Byron, yes, yes, yes!"

Pleasure, ecstasy, delectation poured through her, out of her, and into her, and Nancy almost wept with the intensity of the intimacy as Byron's tongue brought her to climax.

When the pleasure started to fade, flickering in her breasts and the ache in her stomach longer than anywhere else, Nancy felt movement. She managed to open her eyes as Byron appeared from out of her skirts.

"That…that was—"

"Dear God, I could do that to you every day for the rest of

your life," Byron breathed, his face warm and his eyes eager.

What on earth could possibly come next?

"That was—why did you..." Nancy swallowed. There was not enough moisture in her mouth, but there certainly was between her legs.

"Nancy, I need you," Byron said quietly. "Come here."

And she went willing into his arms. *Why wouldn't she?* He was everything she wanted, and had proven himself to be a man of honor—and a man of pleasure.

Their eagerness overwhelmed them. Before Nancy knew quite how they had managed it, they were on the bed, Byron's breeches around his ankles and her skirts pushed up, revealing herself.

But she wasn't ashamed. Not after what Byron had already done under her skirts...

"I've got a preservative," Byron muttered in between frantic kisses.

Nancy frowned as his kisses trailed to her breasts. "A—"

"Something to prevent a child," he panted, shifting slightly so that he nestled between her legs. "Are you ready?"

And though she had assumed she would hesitate at this moment, ask him to slow down, give herself time to think—Nancy found she needed no time at all.

"Take me."

Byron needed no further encouragement. With her gown pushed up around her, hardly believing that she had permitted herself to do something so wild, Nancy tensed, ready for the intrusion of his manhood.

And though it was an intrusion, of sorts, it brought none of the pain she had expected. Instead, Nancy felt herself be filled, slowly but surely, with inch after inch as his manhood entered her.

"Oh, Nancy," he groaned.

Nancy felt herself softening, stretching to permit him entrance all the way, and knew she could never share this with anyone else. No other man would ever touch her, certainly not like this. Byron had ruined her, perhaps forever. She would never kiss another man again.

And then he shifted.

"Byron!"

He grinned, concentration etched across his face. "Was—was that good?"

Nancy grinned, trying to ensure he knew she was teasing. "I don't know—you'll have to do it again."

He moved out and in again, and Nancy's back arched by instinct.

"More, I want more!"

The subtle rhythm shifted, growing faster and faster. As Nancy clung onto Byron's shoulders, hardly able to see, such pleasure was roaring through her, she recognized it. It was the same rhythm that he had wrought against her secret place with his tongue, and before long, she knew what heady delights lay in store.

And perhaps the mere thought pushed her over the edge.

"Oh God, yes!"

"Nancy, Nancy!"

And whether it was her pleasure, the throbbing twisting shudder in her, or the way she cried out, Nancy did not know.

All she knew was that Byron suddenly pounded into her, releasing himself from all constraints, and he shuddered as he fell first into her arms, and then slipped from her embrace to lie beside her.

Nancy tried to slow her breathing, but swiftly gave up and merely embraced the rush of excitement and wonder that was filling her.

Well, she had done it. She had decided it was time to lose her innocence, and she had given it to a man who certainly knew how to please a woman, despite his professed inexperience.

The question was…what were they going to do now?

CHAPTER FIFTEEN

September 9, 1810

T HE GLINT OF dawning sunlight on the spoon was absolutely transfixing Byron.

He turned it over slowly. The shine on the cutlery glittered around the room, throwing sparks of light. Byron continued to turn it leisurely. The light fell onto a woman.

Nancy blinked, smiling at the brightness. "Byron!"

He grinned, unable to help himself. It was such a small thing. A shining light, probably no bigger than a shilling. As he moved it about, he made Nancy blink in wonder at the way the piece of metal shimmered.

Those dark red eyelashes, fluttering in the early morning air. Her hair, barely pinned now, each successive evening leaving her with fewer and fewer pins as her curls cascaded past her shoulders. The soft flush of her cheeks.

Byron's stomach stirred. Well, perhaps lower than his stomach.

"Breakfast will be out shortly," said a voice just to his left.

Jerking his head, Byron saw a serving maid bob a curtsey and disappear. The dining area of this inn was almost empty—a surprise at first, as the quality of the place seemed so high. But then, as Nancy pointed out, it was very early.

"Nearly six o'clock," Byron said aloud. "We should be gone by seven."

She nodded, lifting up her cup and taking a sip of tea.

Transfixed was not quite the word. Byron had never been hypnotized—he had only read about it in books or in the more salacious newspapers. But if he could imagine being hypnotized, it was like this.

No matter what he tried to do, no matter where his eyes looked, no matter what train of thought he attempted...it all led back to her. Nancy.

"Was—was that good?"

Byron shivered. Never before could he have guessed...the connection, the intimacy that one built with a woman once they had shared...

"I don't know—you'll have to do it again."

It had been better than he could possibly have imagined. Better than he had hoped.

And now he could look back on it, Byron could not help but admit—at least, in the privacy of his own mind—that he was glad it was her.

Over the years, he'd had opportunities. Every man had. Dukes had more than their fair share. But he had resisted, and at the time he had not known why. If anyone had asked, his articulation might have been something around the fact that it wasn't the right time.

But last night had been.

"Dear God, I could do that to you every day for the rest of your life."

"What are you looking at?"

Byron started. His gaze had evidently taken on a vague, unfocused look, for Nancy was flushing all the deeper and looking at her hands on the pristine white tablecloth.

He could lie. Dissemble. Attempt charm. Perhaps the Duke of Sedley would have.

But today, he was just Byron Renwick. *For one last day.* "You, of course."

"Why?" asked Nancy swiftly, raising a hand to her cheek.

Byron swallowed. *Did she have any idea how beautiful she was?* Probably not. Truly beautiful women who were cognizant of the effect they had on men did not barge into gentlemen's carriages. Even ones desperate to save sisters.

No, Nancy had never heard, not before last night, just how alluring she was. How she tempted him. How she must torment any man who came within half a mile of her...

Oh, the very thought of dragging his gaze away, it was agony! Byron knew, deep within him, that losing her—

"You have to stop looking at me," said Nancy shyly, twisting her head as though avoiding his gaze could remove it.

Byron chuckled. *The very idea.* "I can't stop looking at you."

"Well, you have to," she shot back with a wry smile, finally meeting his gaze.

His heart skipped a beat. "Why?"

"Because breakfast is here," Nancy said sweetly.

Byron twisted in his seat to see the serving maid return with two plates covered in what appeared to be hot, steaming bacon and eggs.

His stomach growled, but it wasn't the only part of him that hungered. "Damnit, I know what I'd rather eat."

As he turned back to the table, he saw Nancy's cheeks were absolutely scarlet. His stomach swooped. Oh, to think of what he would have said if they were alone...

But he would have to wait until they were back in the carriage before he could say what was in his heart. Or do what he wanted to do her right now.

"You're going to have to look at your breakfast sometime," Nancy pointed out.

Byron blinked. She had already begun eating, but he couldn't find the will to pick up his cutlery. To eat would bring them closer to getting back in the carriage, finding the mail coach, and...

He had spent so long thinking about how he would bring the Glasshand Gang to justice, it was only now he realized that afterward was...emptiness. Nothing. He had not thought beyond that moment in so long, it was difficult to imagine what it could contain.

"You're still looking at me, you know."

Byron nodded, his face serious. "Yes, I cannot stop looking at...at my wife."

Nancy colored, quickly taking a sip of tea as though that would prevent him from noticing. She said nothing.

The words tasted unusual in his mouth, but not unwanted.

And it came to him, sharp and true, the knowledge of what he would do after the Glasshand Gang were successfully handed over to London, to Snee.

He would marry Nancy Mead.

Byron's heart twitched in his chest, but it was not rebelling, merely agreeing. Marrying Nancy; yes, that was what he wanted.

And why not? The duchy needed heirs, and it was high time he got to the business of making them. And Nancy was...Nancy. Everything. Witty, clever, kind, bold. Beautiful. Everything a duchess offered—at least, everything he had hoped, in the vagueness of youth, his future bride would be.

Perhaps if his father had lived, there would have been an organized match, an arranged marriage. A wry grin slid over Byron's lips. Miss Ashbrooke would have been called, and that would be the end of it.

But his father was gone. That left him chained to a vow to bring down the Glasshand Gang, but also...free. Free to marry whoever he wanted. Free to offer matrimony to Nancy.

"You're thinking about something," she stated.

Byron grinned. "Now, I can't help that, can I?"

He leaned forward and took in a mouthful of delicious bacon. He would need to be prepared for a busy day—particularly busy, if his suppositions were correct and they would catch up with the Glasshand Gang today.

"Should we be rushing?" Nancy said anxiously.

The thought had occurred to him, but Byron shook his head. "They're human, just like we are. They'll have to stop for food, drink—and their passengers will demand frequent stops. Their horses will need changing. We can sit here a while. Together."

Together. It had a rather nice ring to it. Byron wondered whether Nancy noticed the way his tongue twisted on that particular word, wishing to hold onto it for as long as possible.

She smiled, her gaze flickering down as her body shivered. Not because of the temperature of the room. Despite the autumnal day, it was pleasant in here.

Byron's chest tightened with pride. It was because of him. She cared—perhaps even loved him. And even if she didn't now, she would. When she discovered he was a duke—he would have to think of the right time to tell her, obviously—she would fall into his arms and give him anything he wanted.

After all, what woman would be able to deny a duke?

"So, what will you do when we catch them?"

Byron blinked. "Them?"

What on earth was she talking about?

Nancy stifled a laugh, glancing at the other guests of the inn who were starting to descend into the dining area. "The Glasshand Gang, of course, you ninny."

Byron smiled weakly. *Ah. Yes.* Strange, how swiftly he could forget the sole reason he had started out on this journey.

The trouble was, it hadn't stayed that way for long. The moment he had started to talk to the woman opposite him, things like purpose and vows started to fade into the background. Not entirely, enough to keep him going.

But sufficient to distract him when faced with a beautiful woman.

"Goodness, I thought you could not stop thinking about the Glasshand Gang for ten minutes together," Nancy was saying, finishing the last of her tea. "After everything that has happened between you and them…"

Byron's chest tightened painfully, tension ripping along his shoulders. She couldn't know, could she? There was no possibility that she could actually know.

He had been so careful. The words had never slipped through his lips, he had been sure of that. And as she didn't know his full name, his true name, there was no possibility that she had heard about it before—perhaps read about it?

And yet she was looking at him as though her words were obvious, as though she had stated nothing more than the truth.

When Byron tried to speak, his voice was hoarse. "What…what do you mean?"

"Well, your father, of course," said Nancy in a low voice, nothing but sympathy and kindness. "After the loss you have suffered, I would have thought—"

"Oh, my father, yes," Byron said hastily.

She did not know, then. Of course she didn't. He had taken great pains to ensure that particular piece of information had never left the family. And if he had his way, it never would. The whole scandal could be carefully hidden. No one but Snee would have to know…

"So, after we have caught them," continued Nancy, utterly oblivious to the turmoil within him. "What will you do?"

"Do," repeated Byron, as though that would answer the question. "Do…"

Truth be told, when he looked into the future, all he saw was her. Nancy at his table, entertaining guests with wit and charm. Nancy, riding alongside him in the open countryside, hair flying in the wind and a laugh on the breeze. Nancy, lying in bed beside him, beckoning him with willing arms…

"Byron? Byron, are you quite well?"

Byron cleared his throat. "Quite well."

"Except you've gone all red," Nancy continued, peering closely and making further heat rush to his cheeks. "Goodness, you look most uncomfortable. Are you—"

"Entirely well, I thank you," he said.

Lord, it was going to be a fine thing if he couldn't control himself around this woman! What had she done to him? Why was it so difficult to concentrate?

"Thank you," Byron said quietly. "For last night."

Now it was Nancy's turn to blush.

He had not said the words to shame her, far from it. The sentiment had been bubbling underneath the surface for some time, and it felt only natural to speak it aloud. *Last night.*

Could he ever have imagined such intimacy? Could he have believed in such depth of emotion, tied with such heights of pleasure?

"I...I hope you do not regret it."

Byron's mouth fell open. "Regret it?"

Nancy was not meeting his gaze, her hand twisting her fork on her now empty plate. The scrape of the metal on the china etched at his ears.

Regret it? "How could you think I would—"

"Because I would not blame you if you did," Nancy said in a rush, still not looking at him. "There are plenty of gentlemen who agree to such a thing then wish they had never—"

"You think I could regret something so wonderful?" Byron said in amazement, struggling to keep his voice down.

Other guests of the inn glanced over and he fought the instinct to snap that they shouldn't be staring at their betters. *No one here knows you are a duke,* he tried to remind himself. *And you need to keep it that way. Just for a few more hours.*

"Last night was special," Byron said quietly, as Nancy did not say anything. "More special than I could ever have hoped, and you—"

"I will understand if you were not pleased with—"

"Will you let me get a word in edgewise, woman, and tell you how much I care about you?" Byron snapped.

The words had left his mouth before he could censure them, but he wasn't completely sure he would have. They felt natural, honest. Perhaps the most honest he had been with Nancy since the first moment they had met.

Byron swallowed. Well, it wasn't as though their entire acquaintance was built on lies. Just...just some half-truths. And he would make it right, he told himself sternly as Nancy continued to be silent. Everything would be made right once he revealed himself to Nancy, told her he was a duke, and asked for her hand.

Once they had caught the Glasshand Gang.

"I just...I did not want you to be disappointed," came Nancy's half-whispered words.

And Byron acted on instinct. Reaching across the table, he took her unresisting hands in his and held her fingers tightly. Her pulse throbbed beneath his own, strong and insistent.

He forced himself to look into her eyes. There was fear there. And pain, pain of loss. Rejection. He could read her so clearly, he almost gasped. Nancy had opened herself to him, and he had been so focused on his own dramatic transformation, his own loss of innocence, that he had not adequately considered hers.

Well, that stopped now.

"Nancy Mead," Byron said quietly. "Last night was the most special—"

"You don't have to say—"

"I speak only the truth, and it's important for you to hear," he cut in with a wry smile. "I have the impression you rarely hear praise of your own merit, and Nancy, last night was..."

Byron's voice trailed away as he attempted to think of how to explain it. A meeting of minds, of bodies, of desires. Exquisite pleasure, yes, but the safety and intimacy of her arms was what he remembered the most.

But how could he explain, sitting here having breakfast with others all around them?

"Even if I could go back in time, once, twice, nine times," Byron said quietly, "I would never change what happened last night. It was perfect—you were perfect. And I never want that to change. I never want to be with another—"

He caught himself just in time, but seeing the look of surprise and delight in Nancy's eyes, it was not just quick enough.

Well, his timing wasn't always perfect. And it wouldn't hurt her to know his intentions, even obliquely. He would marry her. Just not yet.

"Well, I am glad," Nancy said softly, her fingers tightening around his. "Because for me, it was...everything."

Affection swelled in Byron's chest as he looked at her. Nancy. His Nancy. After today, they would never have to be apart—but they should probably pretend not to know.

It would not do, after all, to get ahead of themselves. Even if a future without her was unbearably dull and empty.

"Well," he said, removing his hand.

Nancy smiled as she slipped her hands back to her lap. "Well."

They sat in silence for a moment. Byron rested in it, knowing he did not have to speak. It was odd; as a duke, the silence was always filled by someone. Someone looking to impress, to recommend a daughter to him, or ask him to speak on behalf of a son—usually to get acceptance into the Dulverton Club.

But here, with Nancy, in an inn on a Kentish road, they could just sit. Happy in each other's company. Had anyone else discovered this? Or was this something special of their own?

"We should probably get going."

Byron nodded. She was right. Sitting here for the last five minutes had been pleasant, but the rest of the day would not be. They had to get onto the road, find the Glasshand Gang, and bring them to justice. Finally. After all this time.

"And then when we are back in London," Nancy said airily, rising from her seat. "You may find you end up in my part of the city. My very street, perhaps."

Byron grinned as he rose too. "Oh, might I?"

"You never know," she said with a laugh. "Your business surely takes you all over London, does it not?"

His stomach twisted. "Yes, I suppose it does."

"Well then, if you should ever wish to visit..." Nancy stepped out of the inn into the blinking new dawn. "I am sure I would be pleased to see you. Very pleased. You could stay for dinner."

Happiness such as he had never known radiated through Byron's chest as he slipped her hand into his. "Careful. Issue invitations like that, and I may never leave."

Nancy steadily met his eye. "Well. That wouldn't be the end of the world, would it?"

CHAPTER SIXTEEN

N ANCY LOOKED AT the man who had not only taken her innocence, but her very heart, and knew she could never be apart from him. She would be his mistress rather than return to London and never see him again.

But did he feel that too? As they sat here over the remnants of their breakfast, could he understand the depths of emotion she felt for him? Was last night truly as wonderful for him as it had been for her?

"Dear God, I could do that to you every day for the rest of your life."

Nancy swallowed. *It had just been one night.* Though they had taken precautions, she would know in a few weeks if there were any…lingering consequences.

And in a way, she hoped there were. She wanted a connection to Byron, a part of his heart, his soul, his very life.

The idea of never seeing him again…

Well, that simply meant she had to be a little more direct in her approach, she thought, steeling herself to say the words she knew would provoke a reaction, one way or the other. It was better to know, wasn't it? Really know?

"And then when we are back in London," Nancy began, as nonchalantly as she could manage. She rose from her seat, indicating they should be going. "You may find you end up in my part of the city. My very street, perhaps."

She saw a slow grin slip across Byron's face as he also rose. "Oh, might I?"

Nancy's heart skipped a beat. If he had no intention of ever seeing her again, he would not have said that, would he?

Not with that jovial air. Not with a smile, a laugh, an acknowledgement unsaid but clear. They were speaking of something more.

"You never know. Your business surely takes you all over London, does it not?"

His business. Had he ever mentioned what it was? For the life of her, she could not recall if he had—but then, the way his mouth had worked on her body yesterday, it would not be surprising if her memory had slipped.

Goodness, the thought of sharing that again in the carriage…

"Yes, I suppose it does."

"Well then," said Nancy as they walked toward the door past the other guests breaking their fast. "If you should ever wish to visit, I am sure I would be pleased to see you. Very pleased. You could stay for dinner."

The dawn, though early, was painfully bright as they stepped outside. Nancy blinked, attempting to help her eyes acclimate to the light.

A new day. The day, in fact, in which their entire purpose for leaving London would finally be fulfilled. They would find the mail coach, she would rescue her sister, and Byron would find the retribution and justice he so sorely craved.

Nancy's stomach lurched. And then it would be over.

But those reasons weren't the only purposes driving them forward anymore, were they?

No, if she was honest with herself, they hadn't been for a long time. She wanted to be with him. Being with him gave her such happiness, such joy…Nancy could not explain it, even if she were bold enough to try.

"Careful. Issue invitations like that, and I may never leave."

Nancy's heart leapt for joy as she met his eyes. *He loved her.* He hadn't said the words, not precisely, but that did not matter, did it? She knew what he meant. Gentlemen were hardly the most open with their hearts. Words were important, yes, but actions? They were the most important thing.

And Byron had acted.

"Well," she said briskly, thinking of Byron moving into their rooms in London, the joy it would bring her to see him every day. "That wouldn't be the end of the world, would it?"

Byron grinned. His hand had taken hers and there was nothing more that she wanted. The day was here; they were going to find Beth, and—

"All we have to do now is find the carriage," Byron said with a dry laugh. "I would have thought Campion would have it ready by now."

Nancy looked around. He was right. Now that she came to think about it, the few nights they had spent on the road, his driver always had the carriage prepared for them, horses chomping at the bit to get away.

But the inn yard was empty. Oh, there were a few people milling about, a baker stepping across, his wares in his arms. A milkmaid, pails over her shoulders. Other than that, the place was unoccupied.

"That's odd," said Nancy slowly.

She could feel the change in him. The tension. The uncertainty. Even if she had not been holding his hand, she would have felt the shifting panic rising in Byron's chest.

Glancing at him, Nancy saw her instincts were right. Byron's brow had furrowed, and his eyes had that unhappy, hopeless look.

An instinct to protect him, care for him, overwhelmed her— tempered by another emotion, one rarely found in her heart. Pride—pride that here was a man who could take care of himself.

Byron wasn't anything like Matthew. She wouldn't have to spend the rest of her life with Byron wondering whether he would accidentally run up a debt, worrying he would make a promise to another he couldn't keep.

Byron was—

"And where is Campion?" Byron said, concern in his voice. "Where is the carriage?"

"The carriage isn't here, and neither is he. We must presume they are together," Nancy said quietly.

Byron dropped her hand. "But the man would never take the carriage off and—he would know we need it here!"

Nancy swallowed. She liked Campion, from what she knew of him, but had interacted with enough servants to know what someone could be pushed to if they were pushed too far.

Though she hated to even consider it, she had to voice the likely possibility of what had occurred.

"Do you think...is there any chance he might have..." she began timidly.

She halted the moment Byron met her eye. "Campion would never do such a thing. He wouldn't be such a fool, regardless of his loyalty to me, and to my house. He would not steal my carriage. That's all."

Byron stomped toward the stables. Nancy stared after him.

His house? What a strange way to put it—almost the sort of thing a royal prince would say, or a duke. She laughed in the cold, brisk air. Well, everyone had their own unique turns of phrase, she supposed. There was still time to learn Byron's.

When she caught up with him, Byron had stepped into the stables with a glower.

"Campion!"

Nancy gasped in horror. "Campion!"

The man did not respond. It was rather difficult to reply when one was bound and gagged.

Nancy did not think, she just acted on instinct. "Campion!"

"Nancy, wait!"

But she did not heed Byron's warning. How could she just stand there, looking at a man beaten badly, lying in the straw in a most painful and awkward position? All thoughts of her own safety, the fact there could be miscreants still in the stables—they disappeared.

Nancy knew what she did best, and that was caring for others. Campion looked badly hurt.

"Campion, what happened?" she said, dropping to her knees and pulling the rag from his mouth.

The driver spat, trying desperately to swallow as his hoarse voice made sounds, but nothing that could be understood as words.

There were heavy footsteps and a muttered curse. Nancy looked up to see Byron beside her, crouching over his servant with a look of devastated concern.

And in that moment, she loved him more. Here was a man who had sufficient coin to merely purchase another carriage. Servants must come in and out of his life like water. It would be easy to chastise the man, criticize him for losing such a precious thing as a carriage.

Yet all Nancy could see in Byron's eyes was concern.

Oh, that she could capture the heart of such a man!

"Slowly there, Campion, we're in no rush," came Byron's quiet voice. "Swallow. You'll get there."

The driver tried to clear his throat again, and this time, his words were audible. "We've been robbed!"

Nancy tried not to smile. Well, obviously. The question was, by whom?

It appeared Byron did not need to consider the question. "The Glasshand Gang!"

"Why would they—"

"Oh, they must know that we're onto them!" Byron said angrily, straightening up and pacing around the stable, kicking up straw. "Why else would they change their route? Everyone knows the Dover Road is the quickest route."

Nancy nodded helplessly. Well, there was no point in attempting to disagree with him.

"And here they were, ready and waiting," Byron barked bitterly. "What, did they jump out at you, Campion?"

"I was asleep; the innkeeper said I could bed down here as it was to be a cold night," rasped the driver. "I was awoken suddenly by a great club to the head; they already had my hands, I couldn't—"

"No one blames you," Nancy soothed, attempting to untie the knots cutting into his wrists. "*Are* they, Byron?"

Her pointed statement got the man's attention. "I beg your pardon? Oh no, not at all. You were overcome, Campion, there's no shame in that."

"But the carriage—"

"The carriage is gone," Byron said ruefully. "Oh, blast it."

Nancy's heart sank as she pulled the rope away from the man's hands. *Yes, blast it.* If she had been a man, she would certainly have sworn in such a manner—or worse.

It was a devastating blow. On the very day they were certain to catch up with the Glasshand Gang, they were foiled—and one of their number badly hurt. That was a nasty cut above Campion's eye. He would need to get it looked at.

And worse of all—

"They'll be arriving in Dover in just a few hours!" Byron exploded, his painful frustration evidently unable to be contained. "To think, we were so close!"

"It is not the end of the world," said Nancy quietly.

He spun, glaring. "Not the end of the—it may have escaped your notice, Nancy, but we have no carriage!"

"But we do have horses."

"And yes, it wasn't my best carriage, but that is hardly the point!" Byron continued, evidently not listening. "I mean, I had the blasted thing painted only last month! It's worth at least—"

Rising slowly to her feet, Nancy stepped away from Campion who was now attempting to untie the knots around his ankles.

There were ten stable bays here. Most were empty. One at the end held a cart horse that might belong to the inn itself. But beside it...

"—and we were so close!" Byron was bemoaning, still strid-ing around the stable in a temper. "So close! My father would be so disappointed if he thought I had given up so quickly, but what can I—"

"I said we have horses, Byron," Nancy breathed, looking up into the majestic eyes of one of the carriage horses.

He nickered gently, his companion on his right peering over to see what all the fuss was about.

Nancy's heart soared. It wasn't all lost then. There was a chance, even if it was slim, that they could rescue Beth. Prevent her from being another casualty of the Glasshand Gang's terrible crimes.

And all she had to do was get Byron to listen for more than five seconds together...

"—no carriage here we could hire, of course!" Byron said, throwing up his hands. "That would be too easy! If we only had—"

"Your Grace," murmured Campion.

Nancy blinked. She must have misheard that—the man's voice was hoarse, still sore from all the shouting he must have done in the night while attempting to raise help. She must have dreamed it. She had, after all, slept very little.

A wry smile crept across her face. Something she could blame on the man still pacing like a caged animal.

"—and how I'll ever face Snee, I don't—"

"Byron!"

He halted, face like thunder, and snapped, "We've been robbed!"

"I know," said Nancy gently, opening the pens and leading out the two horses.

"It's outrageous!"

"It certainly is," she said gravely, trying not to smile. "And it would be most injurious to our plans, if not for—"

"I simply cannot think what we—hang on," said Byron in wonder, stepping forward with wide eyes, as though he had only recently been gifted the power of sight. "We have horses."

Nancy grinned. "I did say we have horses."

Byron reached out to stroke the nose of one, then turned to her and said in a stronger voice, "We have horses."

"That we do."

"I just don't understand how they found us," said Byron darkly. "Unless…"

Nancy blinked under the ferocity of his gaze. "What are—"

"Unless one of us is secretly working for the Glasshand Gang."

Her mouth fell open. Well, of all the outrageous things to say! "You cannot be serious."

"Deadly," said Byron, his gaze unwavering. "After all, you could have sent messages to them. Given them clues as to—"

"Why would I do that when they threaten my very sister's life?" Nancy said hotly.

Really, it was absurd! But there was a strange sort of light in Byron's eyes, as though he was finally seeing something clearly for the first time. And fear entered her heart. Was it possible that after all they had shared, he could suspect her of such a heinous thing?

"Byron Renwick, why would I be a part of the Glasshand Gang?" Nancy said as stiffly as she could manage. "They are abhorrent, awful, criminals! All I want is to see my sister safe and…and perhaps spend a little more time with you."

It was painful to admit to such a thing in the middle of what had somehow become an argument, but Nancy could not help it. The idea that Byron would accuse her of such a thing…

And suddenly, the cloud which had overshadowed Byron's face cleared. He blinked, as though coming to himself.

"Foolish of me. I apologize, Nancy," he said, far more formally than she had expected. "In the heat of the moment, I—forgive me."

"I don't want to worry anyone," came a voice from behind Byron. "But I think my ankle is broken."

Byron spun around.

Nancy stepped forward, apprehension welling in her chest. "Are you sure?"

"Well, I am no doctor," said Campion, and Nancy saw with concern that his face was pale. "But I cannot put any weight on it. I'll be no help to you from here on in, I am afraid."

"They are callous," she breathed, forcing herself not to look at the man's ankle. She didn't think she would faint, but she didn't want to risk it.

This Glasshand Gang...she had always known they were dangerous. Anyone who read the newspapers in London knew it.

But to see the evidence before her, to know they had attacked an innocent sleeping man who had no chance to defend himself! That was the sort of person who would soon be attacking the mail coach within which her sister sat.

Nancy bit her lip and looked at Byron.

It was wonderful, having someone to turn to in a crisis. How long had it been since she could honestly say there was someone else in the room that could be depended on?

Perhaps that was too harsh on Matthew and Beth; they had been young when their parents had died, and she would not have liked them to carry the burden of responsibility.

She had been crying out for someone to stand alongside her in the most challenging of moments. And here he was.

Byron was still silent. Nancy's heart sank. Well, she was always happy to take action when needed.

The moment she opened her mouth, Byron spoke.

"We'll get you up to the inn, find you a room, and call a doctor," he said firmly. "There is absolutely no way we would ask you to come with us, not in this state. Right, Nancy?"

Nancy nodded vigorously. "Of course. You'll have to rest up, Campion, and then once we've caught the Glasshand Gang—"

"You're not seriously thinking of taking her with you?" asked Campion.

Nancy blinked. *Now what on earth did that mean?* They only

had two horses, after all. How could they—

"Nancy can look after herself," Byron said, looking sharply at his servant.

"But Your—".

"I have made my decision—at least, Nancy has made hers, I think," Byron added hastily, turning to her. "Well?"

Nancy swallowed, heart racing. This felt like an important moment, one she would never see again. A chance to make a decision, it appeared…but what?

"What are you asking me?"

Byron smiled, taking her hands in his. She flushed, conscious the driver was but a few feet from them. But it felt so natural. As though this was what they should spend the rest of their life doing.

"I am going to Dover today, and I fully intend to meet with the Glasshand Gang," Byron said. "Either on the road or in Dover itself. There will be fighting, probably. It might be dangerous."

Nancy swallowed. She wasn't sure what was filling her stomach with fear the most: the thought of having to fight, the idea of Byron in danger, or the thought that Beth still had no idea just how hazardous her position was.

But merely waiting here at the inn with Campion…waiting for news, hoping two of the three people she loved most in the world would escape danger just a few miles away…

"I'm coming with you," Nancy stated.

Byron grinned. His smile rushed warmth through her, bathing her in a golden light that could not be seen, only felt. She would be safe with him, she knew that. And she could be in danger staying here—if the Glasshand Gang knew they had been staying here last night…

"They say that a stitch in time saves nine," she said quietly, squeezing his hands. "There are nine people on that mail coach. One of them means a great deal to me."

Byron nodded. "We have to save everyone on that mail coach."

"And we will," Nancy said. She could see the need in him, the determination to finish what he had started all that time ago. "And we have the horses."

His gaze left hers, just for a moment, as he glanced at them. When he looked back at her, there was a gentle worry in his eyes. "And you are sure you can ride?"

Nancy hesitated. She had not ridden for...oh, ten years? Maybe more? It had been difficult to justify keeping the horses, her mother had said, as they had such little greenery around them to enjoy. Nancy and Matthew had never ridden.

It was only when she had grown older that she had realized, with the benefit of hindsight and maturity, that it wasn't the lack of greenery. They simply had been unable to afford them.

But there were some things one never forgot. How difficult could riding a horse be?

"You'll have to ride bareback," added Byron, as though reading her thoughts. "No side saddle, no saddle at all."

Nancy swallowed as nerves crashed into her heart. Could she do it? Would she ruin everything by attempting it, hold Byron back as he needed to get to Dover?

And then he squeezed her hand.

Certainty, absolute certainty that he would aid her, support her, and ensure they both reached the mail coach in time rushed through her.

Nancy grinned. "Of course I can ride, no problem there. The question is, will you be able to keep up?"

CHAPTER SEVENTEEN

I T WAS WITH a strange mingling of panic, excitement, and adoration for the woman riding beside him that Byron set out. He could only imagine it was going to get more complicated.

After all, he was not sure he had made the right decision. Perhaps Campion had been correct. Perhaps it was a mistake to even think about bringing Nancy with him.

"You're not seriously thinking of taking her with you?"

"We could spend all day looking for them on the roads," Nancy had cleverly pointed out as they had set off. "Surely it is better to simply go to where we know they will be?"

Byron had, for just a moment, wished he had thought of that. Then he had pushed the thought aside and allowed himself to feel pride in the woman he was caring about more and more with each passing moment.

Her cleverness did not detract from his own character. It was a strange lesson to learn, but one he hoped would keep them both happy in the future.

The future.

Byron smiled as he and Nancy galloped through the Kentish countryside. How had he never noticed the beauty of nature before? The tall, majestic trees which reached to the heavens, blessing the earth with their golden leaves. The hedgerows, bright and bursting with berries, chattering with the noise of birds. The glorious fields, stretching out before them, and around them, rolling downs of green and gold.

A lump caught in his throat. The world was so beautiful. Was it Nancy's presence which helped him to see it? Or was it something else? Was it his love of Nancy? For love it was, he could not deny. Was it finding love that had opened his eyes to wonder all around him?

"You're very quiet."

"I am unaccustomed to all this riding," said Byron, not entirely truthful, grinning at the beaming woman beside him.

Riding suited her, throwing a delicate beauty over the woman who was already far more elegant than he could have imagined.

Nancy's hair had lost all its pins now, red locks flowing down her back. Her pelisse, slightly worn, suited their adventurous riding. Her cheeks were flushed in the chilly breeze, her lips just as red, begging him to—

Byron swallowed. There would be plenty of time for that later. This time tomorrow, he told himself, it would be over. He would have caught the Glasshand Gang. All of them. Especially—

The important thing was, they'd be behind bars, Byron thought darkly. Where they deserved to be. He would send word to Snee in London; he could be here in a few days.

And it would be over.

"You know, I'm starving," said Nancy unexpectedly.

Byron barked a laugh. "You had breakfast not a few hours ago!"

"Riding is hearty work!" she pointed out defensively, though the smile on her lips told him she was not offended. "Besides, you can't tell me you're not hungry either."

He was certainly hungry, but it wasn't his stomach.

Nancy seemed to know. Her cheeks flushed. "I meant—"

"I know what you meant," said Byron with a laugh. "And goodness, am I going to make you pay for that remark later."

He spoke so swiftly he could not have prevented the words if he tried—and perhaps if he had spoken to a different woman, he would have been mortified.

But Nancy simply laughed as their horses continued along the road. "You had better watch out, Byron, or you'll be the one paying for it!"

Oh, to think that some people actually tired of their wives! Byron could hardly wait to get her back underneath him, let alone walking up an altar.

His heart skipped a beat. The thought of making vows, promises to any woman...it had never appealed. He had never met a woman to make the endeavor worthwhile.

Now he had. Now he had something to lose. His heart was vulnerable, as it had been when his father had lived, but somehow, Byron knew that this would be different. He was not about to lose Nancy to the Glasshand Gang, he told himself fiercely as the road meandered into a small village. He would never lose her.

"We have no time to stop for luncheon," Byron warned.

But it was too late—not for Nancy, but for him. As they trotted along a street, taking care not to get in the way of a large cart horse pulling a dog cart of hay, the heady smells of a bakery wafted through the air.

Nancy breathed in deeply beside him. "Just a quick—"

"We really wanted to get to Dover by the afternoon," he pointed out, though his stomach undermined him by gurgling loudly.

She giggled. "I think you have been outvoted, you know."

Byron sighed, rolling his eyes dramatically, but winking just in case she thought him serious. "Fine—a very swift stop and we'll be on our way. A short one, mind!"

The trouble was, nothing was that simple. It took a few minutes to find the bakery itself, set back on a side road. Then they had to sort out the horses. Nancy thought they could just be left on the street.

"Who would be so foolish as to steal two such well-cared-for steeds?" she said, as though her logic was undeniable. "They would know their owner would search for them—"

"I have already had my carriage stolen from underneath me today," Byron pointed out heavily as he dismounted, reaching out a hand. "No. One of us stays with the horses."

"Fine," said Nancy, slipping from the horse in a rush of silk.

Her hand was clasped tightly in his and he was not standing far from her—which probably explained why her body was suddenly pressed up against his.

Byron took in a deep breath. *A mistake.*

The heady scent of baked pies and bread was immediately overwhelmed by the intoxication of Nancy. She was his, warm and panting after the exertion of their ride, and it was all he could do not to lean down and taste her.

Nancy blinked. "Byron."

Byron groaned. He couldn't help it. He swiftly captured her lips with his, giving himself up to the pleasure of her kiss.

She responded eagerly, throwing her hands around his neck, pulling him closer. Byron knew there was nowhere else he wanted to be in the world than here, in this moment. Every part of him yearned for her. Not just her body and the pleasure they could share together. But her. Her company. Her laughter. The way she challenged him, saw the world differently and was not afraid to point it out.

As the kiss deepened, his tongue meeting hers and a shiver of ecstasy shimmering through him, Byron groaned. "Nancy…"

"Excuse me, sir and miss."

Nancy pulled away, cheeks pink. Byron blinked, dazed from their kiss.

Then he saw, to his shame, they had blocked the pavement due to their unplanned amour.

"Ah," he said helplessly.

"Um," said Nancy.

The man did not give them a second look. He merely walked by, shaking his head.

Byron swallowed, discomfort eating through his stomach. If

this had been London, it would have taken not two hours for the news the Duke of Sedley had been spotted kissing an unknown woman—and on the street, of all places!

The scandal sheets would be up in arms, the gossips of the *ton* would be outraged, and he would surely have been treated to a visit by Lady Romeril to request the return of his vouchers to Almack's.

And if any, or all of those things had occurred, it would have been worth it. Byron would happily undergo such societal outrage for one more kiss with the woman he loved.

Yet here, in whatever village it was they had found themselves in…nothing. No one knew who he was. Not even Nancy.

"We had better get some food," said Nancy breathlessly, looking at the ground. "Quickly, if we are to be back on the road."

Byron nodded. "You go in. Take this, buy whatever you want."

He slipped a few coins into her hands from his pocket and tried not to notice just how uncomfortable the sensation was.

Handing money over to Nancy, just after they had kissed…

Byron pushed the thought away. No, it wasn't like that. Nancy was not just some woman he had bedded and would never see again. Their connection was deeper.

"And what do you want?"

Byron did not think. He answered instinctively. "You."

Nancy flushed as a cool autumnal wind rushed past. "N-No, I meant—well, that's lovely, but I actually meant…"

She pointed at the bakery.

Heat tinged Byron's cheeks. "Oh."

Of course she did. What was he thinking? He needed to concentrate if he was to face the Glasshand Gang in just a few hours. This was not what his father would have expected of him.

And if the person he expected was there…

"Any sort of pie," he said aloud, hoping the color in his cheeks could be argued away by the cold breeze.

Nancy nodded, and still flushed, slipped into the bakery. She returned swiftly with two large brown paper bags.

"Pies?" he asked, taking them as he offered a hand and knee to her.

Nancy nodded as she stepped onto his knee and mounted her horse. "Chicken and mushroom. I hope that is suitable; you did say—"

"At this point, any hot nourishment is more than suitable," Byron said with a reassuring smile, handing the two bags to her as he mounted his own horse. "We'll eat as we ride, if that is agreeable to you?"

Nancy smiled as she offered him one of the pies. "Perfectly agreeable."

And it was rather pleasant, Byron thought. Their horses were walking sedately along the road out of the village, the browning hedgerows on either side of them chittering with birds, still singing as though it were summertime.

The pie was good. Large, hot, and rammed full of chicken— not something you found in the pies one ate in London, if one was foolish enough to eat from a street trader. Byron devoured the thing, not aware of how hungry he was until he reached the last mouthful.

Nancy was giggling. "And you said I couldn't be hungry!"

"It wasn't that," Byron said defensively. "It was—"

"In that case, you won't mind giving me the last morsel of your pie," she teased.

Byron looked at the remnants of his pie, then back at her. Not taking his eyes from the woman who was now laughing, he calmly ate the rest of his pie.

"Outrageous," Nancy laughed.

"Nonsense," he retorted, grinning and wishing every moment could be just like this. Just him and Nancy, a sunny day, and good food. "It's outrageous you didn't buy four pies."

"You honestly think you could have eaten two?"

"I know I could," Byron said wistfully, crumpling up the

brown paper bag and stuffing it in his coat pocket. "It's all this adventuring, it wears out the body!"

"I think it was something else that wore you out last night," came her bold reply.

For a moment, just a moment, Byron watched as Nancy realized what she had said.

He grinned. "You know, I love it when you talk like that."

"What, like a harlot?" muttered Nancy, cheeks red.

Byron shook his head. "As you really think. There is so much censorship in our world, particularly in the circles that I move in."

He had said the words before he had realized what they may suggest.

Nancy giggled. "What, with the lords and ladies you mingle with?"

He tried to smile as their horses rounded a bend. "Yes. Yes, something like that."

Was this it? Was this the perfect time to reveal himself? He had kept the secret of his parentage, of the title and responsibilities he held, for so long. It had almost become second nature between them, and he hated that. Byron did not want deception or lies to become par for the course between him and Nancy.

They were alone. There would be no one else to discover just who he really was…

"Unless one of us is secretly working for the Glasshand Gang."

The memory of the words he had spoken only that morning sparked in his mind, painful and arresting. He had believed her, of course he had. Nancy had denied it, and she would not lie to him.

So why was he still holding back?

"What's the plan then?"

Byron blinked. "Plan?"

The road was more overgrown here. Oak trees on either side spread their branches over the stones, darkening the sky.

"Yes, plan," repeated Nancy. "When we arrive in Dover, what's the plan?"

Byron settled back onto his horse, hardly aware of the tension which had shot up his spine. Perhaps this was best. They needed to finish what they had started, then they could worry about true names and revealing identities.

And making offers of marriage.

"Well, it's simple, really," he said with a deep sigh. "Once the attack has begun—"

"You think we will not arrive in time to stop it?" interrupted Nancy with deep concern.

Byron shrugged. "Even if we do, we cannot. The attack has to begin. Once it does—"

He should have known. He should have realized the moment Nancy's voice changed. All the softness had gone, the sharpness returning as when they had first met.

"What on earth do you mean?" Nancy said sharply. "What do you mean, 'has to begin'? Have we not traveled all this way to prevent it?"

And only then did Byron realize his mistake.

Of course. At no point had he—well, there had been no need to explain before now. For quite a while, he had hardly believed Nancy would still be with him when he caught up with the mail coach, whether on the road or at Dover itself.

Because Snee was right. Byron did not like the fact, but now that he was here, out in the open, without the protection London and his name afforded him, he could not deny it.

"Catch criminals before they have committed a crime? I am not sure whether I can do such a thing, Your Grace."

It was true. Byron had not understood it then. He could not simply walk into Dover and arrest a group of men who, at the time, would have done nothing to merit such stern action.

No, it was not until the Glasshand Gang had started their crime that he could stop them. That was just how it was.

"You see, I can't arrest anyone before they've committed a crime," Byron tried to explain in a calm and reasonable voice as their horses continued to walk along the road. "But once the Glasshand Gang has attacked the mail coach—"

"Attacked the mail coach—are you mad?" cried Nancy, true panic on her face. "I thought the entire purpose of coming here, racing after them, was to stop them attacking at all?"

Byron hesitated, but he had to make her see. It would all be clear, once he had explained. She would understand. "No, because you see—"

"My sister is in there!" Nancy cried, pulling her steed to a halt.

Byron mirrored her, pulling the reins on his horse. His heart cracked as the agony of her face met his eyes.

She was devastated. Not just hurt, angry, more than that. Something Byron had seen once more in the eyes of someone he loved who felt he had not done enough to counter the Glasshand Gang.

Betrayal.

He swallowed. This was not the same as the terrible night his father—this was different!

"You don't understand," he said stiffly. "I made a promise—"

"And so did I, to my sister, to protect her no matter what!" Nancy said, cutting across him with a frown. "And you think just because of your strange rules, I'll watch while my sister risks her life?"

Byron bristled. She had not said the word, but the implication was clear.

Coward.

"This is how justice works! We may not like it, but that is the way it is," he said darkly.

His stomach lurched horribly as Nancy gave a bitter laugh. All the joy, all the understanding between them was gone. "You call it justice, but I call it weakness! I don't care if we catch the Glasshand Gang, I just want to make sure my sister—"

"I must catch them!" said Byron desperately. "I have to! If I don't—"

"I have a sibling on that mail coach, and though you may not understand what it is like to have one, let me tell you—"

And that was what pushed Byron over the edge. He could not

simply sit here on his steed and allow such things to be said to him!

He was a duke. The Duke of Sedley. And a duke who knew precisely what it was to love a sibling. Even though he'd had to harden his heart in recent months.

"You are not the only one with a sibling in Dover!" Byron said, reaching out and grabbing Nancy's hand. She tried to pull away, but he wouldn't let her. "Nancy, my brother is there!"

She stared. "Your...your brother? But you said—a wife, sister, friend, you said, nothing about a—"

"Oh, he's not on the mail coach," Byron said bitterly, hating the truth had to come out now. But there was no choice, was there? "He's...he's with the Glasshand Gang."

Nancy stared in horror as though he had announced a deal with the devil. "The...the Glasshand Gang. And your brother?"

Byron's jaw tightened and he nodded, unable to speak.

So, there it was. Now another soul knew the terrible truth about the brother of the Duke of Sedley—not that she knew the utter disgrace he had brought to the duchy's name. To think, she could tell anyone now. He never would have thought Nancy would, but now he was not so sure.

She pulled her hand from his. "Are you telling me, your brother—"

"Helped rob and kill our father? Yes," Byron spat, hardly able to bear it. Oh, the agony in his chest, when would it end? "And I have to catch him, Nancy, I have to—"

"I understand," she said softly, and for just a moment, Byron was certain everything would be well between them. But then—"But not at the cost of my sister."

"Nancy!"

"No, I am sorry, Byron," Nancy said sternly, eyes cold, all affection he had once seen there gone. "But I cannot sacrifice Beth for a man who would do that. I know he's your brother, but—"

"I made a vow!"

"Then keep it, if you can. But I don't like your type of justice, and I don't like what you're willing to do to stop someone who doesn't deserve your salvation."

"Nancy—Nancy, wait!"

But it was too late. The moment Byron reached for her, desperate to keep Nancy with him, sure if they could just continue their conversation, they could unpick the confusion—

She was gone. Nancy's heels kicked her steed and the horse bolted, moving from a standing start to a full gallop in the blink of an eye.

"Nancy!" Byron called after her desperately, hating the crack in his voice. "Nancy, please!"

She was already out of sight. Likely as not, she could not hear him.

"Oh, God in His Heaven," Byron cursed under his breath.

It had all felt so simple when he had gotten into his carriage in London. Albeit with an unexpected passenger, true, but how much of a difference would that make?

All the difference in the world, it turned out.

Byron took a deep breath. Well, he had a decision to make. The question was, did he have time to make it?

CHAPTER EIGHTEEN

E VERY BREATH ACHED in Nancy's lungs, but she had to keep going. Had to keep breathing. Had to keep forcing her horse forward, further along the road a man a few miles back had called the Dover Road.

Because she could see it. Dover. It had to be, there was surely only one town at the end of the road, nestled into a corner where the land met the sea. She could already hear seagulls crying out, see the ships in the harbor.

The ships that, should all had been well, would have taken Beth to France to save Matthew...

A lump stuck in Nancy's throat and she choked trying to clear it. Her legs ached, every part of her wishing she could just stop, halt the horse, and fall from its back, lie on the damp autumn ground, and catch her breath.

"And I have to catch him, Nancy, I have to—"

Byron's words kept ringing in her mind, echoing, and she could not stop them.

"I understand. But not at the cost of my sister."

Nancy dashed away a tear. She did not have time for tears, for sorrow at the way things had ended between them.

She had been certain they understood each other. That he loved her. That he would comprehend why she had to rush to save her sister, that there was no possibility of allowing anything terrible to happen to her.

But Byron…

"But I don't like your type of justice, and I don't like what you're willing to do to stop someone who doesn't deserve your salvation."

Nancy swallowed hard as the road meandered over a hillock, the town of Dover momentarily disappearing from view. She was almost there. She was almost ready to save Beth—

And then, Nancy vowed to herself in silence as the galloping hooves of her steed filled her ears, she would ensure her sister never left her sight again.

The outskirts of the town welcomed her as people stared with surprised looks.

"Careful there!"

"Where does she think she's going in such a hurry!"

Nancy ignored the pointed stares, the yells, the cries for her to be calm.

How could she be calm? For all she knew, the Dover mail coach had arrived hours ago. It could all be over. The Glasshand Gang could have taken their spoils, injured or even killed the survivors…and that would be it.

She would never see Beth again. Never apologize for permitting her to take the mail coach instead of Nancy. Never hear her voice…

But the trouble was, she had no idea where to go. The streets of Dover were complex, no clear route to the port open, and Nancy was forced to pull on the reins and slow. The horse stamped, breathing hard. Each heavy sigh mirrored her own.

Where was the mail coach?

"You there," she called to a young lad who reminded her forcefully of Matthew when he had been young. "The mail coach?"

He looked up with a scowl. "What's it worth?"

Nancy was greatly tempted to curse under her breath, as Byron was wont to do. But she mustn't think of him. She couldn't think of him, not when she had her sister to consider.

The trouble was, she didn't have any money. No coin on her whatsoever.

"A great deal," she admitted, "but—"

"Ah, no buts," interrupted the boy with a dark scowl. "Information's got a price!"

Nancy tried to take a deep, steadying breath, but it was all she could do not to wrench the lad up by his collar and shake him. How could she have gotten this far, almost reached her destination, and be frustrated here?

"Look," she said desperately, "I—"

"It's that way," said the man passing by with a heavy sigh. "Are you quite alright, Miss?"

Nancy did not have time for proper gratitude. "Thank you, thank you!"

By the time she had reached the third word, she had already kicked her heels into her horse's side. The beast almost reared, but obeyed her command.

Nancy's heart flickered in her chest as the horse took her along the street where the man had pointed.

This was it. The moment she saw whether or not the mail coach was safe. If her sister was...

Nancy's stomach lurched as the smell of salt wafted through the air. Beth had to be safe. Surely she would have felt it, within her, if something had happened to her baby sister?

Oh, she would never forgive herself if she was too late.

Eagerly, she listened, wondering whether she would hear cries or shouts if something had occurred, but all was silence. At least, the silence that filled a small town. Hawking cries as traders attempted to sell, laughter and music coming from a pub further down the road, and with every hoof beat, the rising sound of seagulls...

Then Nancy and her horse burst out onto a promenade. The port. Ships, sails whistling in the wind. The sea.

And along the way, a large coach. *The mail coach.*

Nancy almost fell off the horse in relief. It was here—she had found it. Everything was going to be well, she tried to tell herself. If there had been a problem, she would already see it.

From what she could see, everything was...as it should be. Though the mail coach was about fifty yards along the road so she could not see it in precise detail, there did not appear to be anything amiss. No shouts, no cries, no—and here Nancy had to swallow—no blood on the cobblestones.

She was in time.

The truth of that thought slowly trickled into her mind.

She had made it. She, Nancy Mead, had left London without a second thought, traveled with a man she had thought she could trust and had given herself to...

Nancy shook her head. And the whole time, she thought furiously, slipping exhausted from her steed, she had been certain she would be unable to find Beth. Unable to save her.

If something had happened...oh, Nancy knew she would never forgive herself.

"I should be the one to go."

"And I say you're wrong."

Nancy's jaw tightened with uncontrolled fear as she tried to tie the horse's reins to a nearby post. It had been her fault. She had allowed herself to be persuaded.

But now she could return home with Beth, and they would find another way to retrieve Matthew. A way that put neither of them in mortal danger of being attacked by the Glasshand Gang.

Or falling in love...

Nancy's head jerked up. She did not know why. A noise. A movement. Something.

For a moment, her gaze did not seem to know what to settle on. There were plenty of people milling about the place. The seafront was evidently a popular place. But there was something wrong here, something that was making the hackles on her neck rise.

Something dangerous...

Nancy's gaze fell on a young man, unshaven and with a

gleam in his eye, stepping toward the mail coach. He glanced to his right, and she saw to her horror that dotted throughout the crowd were a number of men in similarly bedraggled clothes.

Each with the same look of glee on their faces.

Nancy's stomach lurched. *Beth.*

"Stop," she breathed, hardly aware she was speaking. "Stop!"

But her shout was carried off by the wind, unheard by anyone save herself—and she needed to move; she had to run forward, warn the two coachmen standing idly by, utterly ignorant of the danger that was approaching them—

So why were her legs stuck to the cobblestones like tar? Why did it take such a tremendous effort to raise her voice?

Panic rushing through her, Nancy tried desperately to move. She had to move—this was her chance, to make it up to Beth, to rescue her, to ensure that nothing terrible happened to her.

Not like it had happened to Byron's father...

"Our house, it was being burgled—our steward was attacked, we could hear it outside, and my father—"

Only then did Nancy truly understand the revenge which had overtaken Byron.

The thought of something happening to Beth, right before her eyes, in the next few awful minutes—how could she ever live with the fact that she was so close but did nothing?

She should have understood, tried to comprehend why he needed to wait.

But it didn't matter now. With horror sinking into her chest, Nancy watched as the Glasshand Gang, scattered amongst the crowd and unheeded by anyone save herself, slowly surrounded the mail coach.

She needed to move!

With a great wrench of effort, Nancy stepped forward.

"Watch out!" she managed to cry, lungs tight as she staggered forward. "Look out there—the Glasshand Gang!"

But her words were caught again by the sea breeze, taken out to the waves and unheard. Nancy knew she had to run, make sure none of them laid a finger on—

"Well, well, well," leered one of the men, reaching the mail coach just as Nancy moved within earshot, her feet dragging. "What do we have in here then?"

She raged with fury, almost weeping with frustration. Nancy knew she was too late, for even if she reached the coach in the next minute, what use would she be? What weapon did she have? What skill had she to keep Beth safe?

She had nothing but her own body, Nancy realized, the terrible dread overcoming her as she saw what had to be done.

"No!" she cried, launching herself forward, energy returning to her limbs as the man reached into the coach with a smirk and tried to pull out one of its inhabitants. "No—"

But she was too late.

That was, too late to reach the man. Because someone else had already done so.

"Unhand her, you ruffian!" cried Byron as he pulled the man back, hard.

The sudden movement unsettled the man. Feet slipping on the sea-sprayed cobbles, the man fell onto the ground with a yelp.

Nancy stared. Where on earth had he come from?

But the fact Byron *was* there was undeniable. There he stood, panting, his face a terrible scowl of anger as he looked around, pulling out a pistol from goodness knew where.

Nancy could barely breathe as she tried to push her way through the now panicking crowd, half of Dover seemingly desperate to flee the scene.

She had to get to Byron—to Beth—to the coach. The three were intertwined now so closely in her mind that she could barely understand what she needed the most.

For them all to be safe, she thought desperately as the Glasshand Gang roared their displeasure at their companion's downfall and rushed forward.

"Byron!" Nancy cried out in fear.

And for a moment, perhaps no longer than a heartbeat, Byron

looked up.

He saw her. Their gazes met. And all sound faded, all movement slowed.

Nancy knew he had seen her, knew she was here to save him just as much as he was to save her. Her love for him, brimming over her heart it was so full, could not be comprehended. And if anything were to happen to him…

And then everything rushed back into focus. There were shouts and cries, the sound of swords being pulled from scabbards, and a shot, a shot in the air!

People screamed, there was a mad rush around her, and for a moment Nancy lost sight of Byron. Was he by the mail coach? Where could he be—and where was Beth?

Nancy's mind solidified to the one thing she could do as fights broke out around her. Byron would be seeking his brother, she tried to remind herself as she was buffeted this way and that. She had to find her sister. Get Beth out of there.

Easier said than done. Nancy had never before imagined what it could be like, standing in a melee of men fighting, and it was nothing to the reality. Shouts and cries, anger, confusion, loud noises and disorientation as everyone continuously moved.

Two men were lying on the ground, and Nancy's heart beat fast as she wondered whether they were Glasshand Gang men or Dover men.

She screamed as she dodged a punch intended for someone else, and just for a moment, she thought she saw Byron look over with panic—but then her view was obscured, and she put out a hand to steady herself and—

The coach. She was standing right by it.

Heart thundering, chest heaving for breaths she so desperately needed, Nancy wrenched open the coach door. "Beth—"

"You won't take me alive!" cried the voice of her baby sister, every tone wracked with terror. "I warn you, I—Nancy?"

Nancy could have wept with relief. There was only one person who spoke like that in a moment of terrible danger. Well, perhaps two. Three, if she included Matthew.

"Come on, we have to get out of here," she said in a rush, reaching out a hand.

Beth's face was pale as she emerged, eyes darting about at the fight around them. "What the—"

"We need to get away, to safety," Nancy repeated, as though saying it in a firmer manner would prevent her sister from asking questions.

She should have known.

"But—"

"I don't have time to explain, Beth, just move!"

Nancy's fingers encircled her sister's and they ran, dodging the men still fighting, her heart pounding. *Where was she going? Where was safe?*

"It's over, Tom!"

Nancy halted so swiftly, her sister accidentally ran into her.

"Nancy, what—"

"Byron," she breathed.

Much had occurred since pulling Beth from the mail coach. There appeared to be only two men left standing now, groaning heaps of men dotting the cobbles.

Byron, a cut just above his eye that was dribbling blood down his cheek...and a man who looked surprisingly similar.

Nancy swallowed. *His brother.*

The man scowled. "You don't get to call me that, Sedley!"

"I can call you what I like!" said Byron calmly, holding out his pistol not quite pointed at his brother.

"Who on earth is this Sedley?" muttered Beth.

Nancy could do nothing but shrug. It wasn't a name she recognized, and was a strange sort of nickname. But she couldn't worry about that. It was the pistol in Byron's brother's hand.

Because that *was* carefully pointed at his brother.

"It's not too late, Tom," Byron said in a low voice. "I have weight with the justices in London, if you would just—"

"You'll never take me alive!" cried his brother.

Nancy could see the agony in Byron's face as he heard those words. She knew, without needing to hear him say it, that Byron had desperately hoped he could save his brother. Save him from the Glasshand Gang. Save him from the hand of justice.

Save him from himself.

But as Nancy could see, not everyone wanted to be saved.

"What, return with you to London in chains, the man who brought such disgrace to the Sedley name?" sneered Byron's brother.

There was that strange name again—but Nancy could not focus on that. Her heart was too busy breaking for the man she loved. If she had ever heard such words spoken in such a way by her brother...

"Aren't you sorry?" cried Byron.

And her heart broke for him, her throat choking up as his brother roared back.

"Of course I am!" said Tom Renwick, his voice cracking. "But I can't—I can't take it back now! I can't change the past—"

"Come with me, Tom," Byron said urgently, taking a hesitant step forward. "We can sort something out, I am sure—"

She gasped at the sudden movement, but Byron was too late. His brother had already stepped back, over the edge and into a waiting boat.

"You come back here!" shouted Byron.

His brother cut away at the ropes keeping it moored to the shore. The heady winds and swift tide meant that, within a moment, the boat was already disappearing off.

"Tom!"

Nancy squeezed her sister's hand. "It's over."

Her words were naught but a whisper. Her shoulders sagged.

It was over. Not her adventure to find Beth. But whatever it was that she and Byron had shared, that was surely over too. He had not reached his man, his brother. His search would continue.

"Nancy?" Beth said uncertainly. "You...you're crying."

Nancy released her sister and raised a hand to her cheeks,

astonished to see moisture on her fingers. "So I am. Well, that's what happens when—"

"Nancy!"

She looked up, heart leaping, to see Byron pushing through the melee. Surely he would not—

"Who is that?" murmured Beth, a teasing grin on her face that made Nancy flush.

"No one."

"No one? Then why is he looking at you like—"

"Nancy, you're safe," said Byron in a rush before pulling her into his arms.

For a moment, Nancy thought she would fight it. Fight the connection, fight the embrace that would surely be their last.

But the instant he touched her, everything changed. She melted into his embrace, his hands tight around her waist, his strong, broad shoulders everything she needed in that moment.

And she knew then. She would never live without him.

"I was wrong," Byron said, his voice muffled as he clung to her. "Oh, Nancy, so wrong, I—"

"Byron, I need to—"

"I realized, the moment I thought you could be there, I knew I would do anything to stop it to keep you safe, justice be damned," Byron continued, his voice breaking. "I would do anything to—"

Nancy was torn, her delight in hearing such words mingled with embarrassment. Her sister was standing right beside her as she was embraced so publicly, and by a stranger! At least, a stranger to Beth...

"And if you would do such a thing for your sister—"

"Byron," Nancy said firmly, pulling herself away from his embrace and wishing to goodness her cheeks were not so hot. "This is my sister."

Byron's gaze flickered from her to Beth. "Ah."

"Byron?" said her sister with a mischievous grin. "Not *the* Byron, surely."

"A cousin," said Nancy and Byron together.

Nancy flushed. She could not have this conversation, say goodbye to Byron forever, in front of her sister!

"Beth, go and stand by the mail coach for a minute while I say…say goodbye to Mr. Renwick," she said stiffly.

Beth narrowed her eyes. "What is going—"

"Please, Beth," Nancy said softly.

Their eyes met, and for once, her sister obeyed without a second argument.

Nancy watched her walk over to the coach and shifted her position slightly so that she could keep her in view. She wasn't about to let Beth meander out of her sight again.

"Say goodbye?" murmured Byron.

Her stomach lurched as she turned to him. "Well, I rather thought…we saved everyone. At least, you saved everyone."

"In time to save nine," he said quietly.

"But now your brother has escaped…"

It was impossible to finish the sentence. How could she? Her voice was breaking just as her heart was. She would have to live with knowing what it was to be loved for just an evening.

Even though her love for him would remain in her heart forever.

"My brother can no longer be my responsibility," Byron said darkly. "I cannot…I will not live my life in his shadow merely because he made the wrong choice. You taught me that."

Nancy swallowed, nerves rushing through her chest. "I did?"

"I was amazed at you running toward the mail coach," said Byron with a wry smile, lifting a hand and pushing back her hair behind her ear. "You were so brave, Nancy."

Oh, it was too much. Just the simplest touch was enough to make her melt. How would she ever live without him?

"Well, people will do anything, I suppose," she breathed, "for the person they love."

Nancy had worried, for a heartbeat, that it wasn't enough. That her words had not sufficiently conveyed all she thought and felt.

Byron acted swiftly, pulling her back into his arms. This time, he poured down kisses onto her lips that were fiery and full of desperate relief.

Nancy responded in kind, clutching him and meeting his kisses with passion of her own. This was what she wanted, Byron, and nothing else. For the rest of her life, even if it meant putting up with whatever business it was he owned, she would love him and protect him. To the very end of her days.

When their kisses finally ended, Nancy laughed to see Byron's red face. "What do you have to be ashamed of, Mr. Renwick?" she teased. "Surely you are not too proud to say you love me?"

"I do love you, Miss Mead," said Byron with a dry laugh. "But I am not Mr. Renwick."

Nancy's heart skipped a beat. "I beg your pardon?"

"I am sorry to say you have not fallen in love with a businessman," he said ruefully.

It was all she could do to keep her face straight. Would she ever truly understand this man? "I haven't?"

"No," said Byron, a smile creeping over his face. "No. You have fallen in love with Byron Renwick, Duke of Sedley."

For a moment, Nancy allowed the words to echo in her ears. Then—

"No, you're not," she said firmly, eyes wide.

Byron grinned. "Absolutely guilty."

He had to be jesting. There was no possibility that he...

And as the truth settled into Nancy's heart, she remembered the signs. His unending wealth, the way people had treated him. The slip up of Campion calling him "Your Grace" just the once. His complete confidence in leaving behind his "business" in London...

The way he looked at her. The way he spoke. The way he had loved her.

Nancy closed her eyes, just for a moment, then started to laugh as she looked at Byron's worried face. "You mean to tell me that I'm in love with a duke?"

"And about to become a duchess, I hope," Byron said quietly.

Nancy threw her arms around him and clung to the man she knew she could not live without. A duke. A duke in time who had saved nine.

CHAPTER NINETEEN

September 20, 1810

B YRON GROANED. "OH, lord…"
  It couldn't be morning. It just couldn't be. Hadn't he only just closed his eyes?

But that was definitely sunlight, liquid gold pouring into the room. Had he left the curtains open? How could he have been so easily distracted?

A warm hand touched his naked back as he lay on his front. Byron grinned, eyes still closed. Perhaps there was one reason he could think of, which gave him far more important things to do than drawing curtains.

"If it is morning already," Byron said, eyes shut against the light. "There is no justice in the world."

A light giggle filled the room, stirring his heart.

Justice. Love. Truth. He had thought he had known what those words meant. He had believed he understood what he had been looking for, the desperate ache in his chest that must be fulfilled.

He had believed Tom would fill that. Either bringing him to justice or welcoming him back into the family. Surely, Byron had believed, his adventure to save nine would have given him one of those two endings.

But it was not to be. Tom had disappeared off from the shoreline, and Byron had been too entangled in the arms of a kiss to notice where he had gone.

And perhaps that was for the best.

Byron blearily opened one eye and saw a woman. Not just any woman. His woman.

Nancy grinned, lying on her side, her red hair a halo in the sunlight. "Good morning."

"Absolutely not," Byron said weakly, closing his eye again. "I refuse to accept that it is morning already!"

"If I could hold back the sun, I would, but I can't," she said with a laugh that made the mattress ripple. "Come on, it surely is not that bad."

Her fingers stroked his back and Byron worked hard to prevent himself from succumbing to the desire already pooling in his stomach.

Would he ever tire of her?

He knew the answer to that question. It would be impossible to tire of a woman so bold yet so unsure of herself. A woman who sacrificed her own safety for those she loved. A woman who had done everything she could to save her sister, and in a way, had saved him, too.

Byron swallowed as Nancy's fingers meandered to his hair, stroking his head and making ripples of longing soar through him.

How had he never noticed the burden of justice upon his shoulders? How had he been unaware of the heavy bulk on his heart, knowing his brother was out there, unrepentant? Perhaps Snee had known. Perhaps that was why he had always made it so difficult to chase after the Glasshand Gang while in London.

But Byron had not recognized it until Nancy had taken him into her arms on that Dover street, and made him happier than he had ever been.

And the weight had gone.

"He's gone," he had said blankly, as Beth had once again joined them, the sea breeze tugging at Nancy's curls.

And Nancy had nodded, held his hand, and squeezed it. "He's no longer your responsibility."

He could have cried out at the shift in his heart. Sometimes, Byron thought, even a week later, he still might. That heaviness was gone, and with it the space in his heart to start something new.

Something he had wanted, even if he had not understood it, the moment he had taken Nancy Mead to her bed.

"You're not falling asleep, are you?"

"If there was any justice in the world, I would be," Byron said in a muffled voice, head still against the pillow.

"Well, the day is still young," came Nancy's teasing voice. "Perhaps we can find a little justice by the time the day is out."

Byron opened his eyes and saw a woman who loved him. Who knew him, all his foibles and complexities and inconsistencies...and loved him. How had he managed it?

"Hello, Nancy," he said quietly.

Nancy replied by pushing him over onto his back and curling up in his arms. "Hello."

They lay there for a moment, Byron glorying in the way she felt. Not just her warmth, the softness of her skin, the subtle way every inch of her movements made him feel alive. But her trust. Her peace. The way she asked nothing of him and gave so much of herself.

Nancy Mead. Not perhaps the name he had expected to make his duchess, but...

"We're living in sin, you know," he said with a teasing air.

Nancy poked him in the stomach.

"Ouch!"

"Well, you deserve it," she said nonchalantly, splaying a hand over where she had so recently unceremoniously poked. "Living in sin, indeed."

"You've stayed here every night since we returned to London," Byron pointed out, heart singing at the closeness they enjoyed. "My servants are probably scandalized."

"Your *servants*," Nancy said with a sigh. "I still can't believe you're a duke, you know."

It had taken rather a lot of getting used to, Byron knew. She had flushed when he was addressed by his formal title, taken a while to acclimatize herself to hearing "the Duke of Sedley" instead of Byron.

For a day, so had he. It had been wonderful, leaving the title behind, merely doing what he wanted, separate from the title.

He had to admit, it was pleasant to be treated like a duke again. Though he would not acknowledge that aloud. He'd had enough ribbing from Nancy's sister in the carriage home.

"You know, if there *was* any justice," came Nancy's sleepy voice, "we would be married by now. Who knew it took so long for banns to be read?"

Byron grinned, arms tightening around the woman he loved.

It was rather irritating, he would admit. Living in sin was one way of putting it; deciding to live in the happiness they were determined to enjoy for the rest of their lives was another.

It amounted to the same thing. The moment he and the Mead sisters had arrived back in London, he'd taken them straight to his townhouse. Wilson, his butler, had been sent around with a few footmen and a maid to clear out their rooms, and they had been immediately moved into the east wing of the house.

To prepare for their nuptials, Byron had said.

No one had complained, though a few of the servants had, he knew, raised eyebrows. Beth had been delighted with her new furnishings, though immediately requested a room for their brother.

"He'll be back before you know it," she had said confidently. "When I go to France to fetch—"

"No, Beth!" both he and Nancy had chimed in.

In a way, they were starting to become a family already. They breakfasted together, spent most of the day planning the wedding or arguing over how to go to France to look for Matthew—Byron was of the opinion he should go, Beth insisted she had to go, and

Nancy declared she would never rest easy if either of them went—and in the evenings, they went their separate ways to their three separate bedchambers.

Byron grinned. *Well. For at least an hour.*

By the time the clocks of the house chimed out midnight, Nancy had always somehow managed to find her way to his bed. To his arms.

"I do love you, you know," he whispered, the words spilling over from the affection in his heart.

Nancy tightened her grip on him, just for a moment. "Of course you do. No one would blame you for falling in love with me."

He snorted. "No returning words of love?"

She prodded him again. "You need me to say them?"

Byron swallowed. "Yes."

It was difficult, this vulnerability lark. He had never thought there'd be much to gain from speaking so openly. His father, his brother, the whole Sedley line, had done very well keeping all emotions pushed far, far down into the depths of their souls.

Never to be seen again.

But Nancy...

She spoke from the heart. Bold, perhaps, but brave, certainly. He was fortunate indeed to find her. To love her. To discover, quite to his surprise, that she truly cared for him.

"Nancy," Byron began.

But before he could continue, she had slipped from his embrace.

"Nancy?"

Byron sat up, grinning at the sight of the utterly naked woman stepping across the bedchamber. Only when he saw what she was about to do did he cry out again.

"Nancy!"

Glancing over her shoulder, red curls cascading past her waist, Nancy grinned. "Time to get up."

"Nancy, what are you—"

With a giggle, she pulled open the curtains. Bright dazzling sunlight poured into the room, the September blue sky sharp against the red of her hair.

Byron groaned, shading his eyes against the astounding light—though not so much that he couldn't see Nancy. "Get away from that window, woman, the whole world will see you!"

And I want you all to myself, he thought with a deep possessiveness he hardly understood. It had overcome him the instant he realized Nancy would have to continue living in a world where there were other men. *Men who could look. Admire. Perhaps even desire...*

Byron's jaw tightened, though it relaxed as she stepped back to the bed and slipped in beside him. He loved Nancy, and that meant trusting her. And it wasn't that he didn't trust her. It was every other brute in the world.

"You know, I'm still catching up on sleep from our ridiculous adventure," he said, pulling her back into his arms.

She giggled. He could feel, as well as hear, her laughter. "It's your own fault, you know."

Byron's eyes widened. "My fault! I suppose you think I should have offered to *buy* every inn we happened to be in, and turn out all the other—"

"No, it's got nothing to do with you being a duke," Nancy said, cutting across him. "And everything to do with the fact that after you kissed me in that first bed—"

"I've already apologized for that!" Byron said hastily.

"My point, if you will let me make it, is that after that night, I would have happily allowed you into my bed," Nancy teased, leaning above him on her elbows.

Byron blinked, hardly able to understand what she was saying. "You...you would?"

Nancy raised an eyebrow. "Your kisses were very persuasive, Byron Renwick. If you'd asked—"

"You mean I could have slept on an actual mattress, stretching myself out across a whole bed, not be scrunched up on a sofa?"

The thought was heady. Oh, to think of all the sleep he had missed...

Nancy tapped him on the nose. "I thought you would be more upset you missed chances to bed me!"

But Byron knew her better than to take her at her word. She had that mischievous air, one that both Mead sisters had and he was learning to understand. If there was any chance the brother was the same, the three of them must have been absolute terrors...

"I am absolutely bereft that I missed out on those two evenings with you in my arms," Byron said with mock severity. "How will I ever overcome the devastation!"

They laughed together. Byron knew he never wanted to be anywhere else, or with anyone else.

The world was right. His world was, at any rate. After months of feeling as though the whole planet was off-kilter, that if he did not do something about it there would never be any rest...now he understood. All he had needed was Nancy.

"Come on, we should get up."

Byron groaned. "I want you here, woman."

"But there's a whole world out there!" Nancy protested. "And besides, my sister will be wondering—"

"Let her," he growled, his fingers moving to her buttocks, his hands cupping them and his voice darkening as wild thoughts rushed through his mind. "My whole world is right here..."

Nancy probably would have responded that a person could not be someone's world—or that he had responsibilities out there—or that they had a meeting later that day with Snee to discuss the potential whereabouts of his brother.

All serious, important things. Things Byron was certain not to miss.

But he couldn't miss this either. He couldn't miss the opportunity to love, and be loved in return.

She had saved him, though Nancy did not know it. Byron

could hardly put it into words, except that he had been lost, and she had rescued him. Though it was a duke who had attempted to save nine lives on that mail coach, in the end, it had been Nancy who had done the saving.

And now, as passion stirred in his loins and Nancy's little whispered moans of pleasure filled his ears, Byron knew there was nothing else he wanted to do but—

"Byron," she breathed.

"Nancy—"

"What do you think our lives would have been if we had not met?"

Byron halted. They were lying side-by-side in his magnificent ducal bed. He had never invited another woman into it, had never felt any sort of deep connection beyond his desire.

But this desire, this need for Nancy, was unlike anything else he had ever felt. Byron could laugh with derision at what his younger self had thought was passion. That was then. This was now.

The thought that their paths may not have crossed…

He may have rushed off to chase after the Dover mail coach without her. He might have asked a completely different person on that night the questions that had led him to Nancy.

It was unthinkable. It was frightening indeed to think such a small chance of fate led him to one person over another.

Byron swallowed. "We would have met."

"But if we hadn't—"

"Somehow, I would have found you," he said firmly. "The thought of not—Nancy, you are everything to me."

Nancy's cheeks flushed pink, a beautiful offset to her red hair. "Truly?"

"My life would be nothing without you, and I am going to spend the rest of my life ensuring you know that. I love you, Nancy."

"And I love you."

"And I very much want to make love to you," he said with a laugh. "Even if I mustn't."

Tendrils of desire were curling once more around his heart. Well, no one could blame him. Byron was certain the sight of Nancy would push any man over the edge. And she was all his...

"Mustn't?" Nancy said archly.

Byron groaned. "Every morning we promise not to lay a hand on each other until we are married, and then every evening—"

"You lay hands on me everywhere," Nancy breathed, her flush deepening.

He swallowed. He was not about to succumb this early in the day. *Probably.* "We have too much of import to do today. Your brother—"

"We will find a way to rescue him, I am sure," she said quietly. "I am just relieved we were in time to rescue my sister."

Byron nodded. The very idea of losing another sibling to the Glasshand Gang...it was not to be borne. Though he'd had to suffer that, he would do much to ensure no one else did.

"Just one more Mead sibling to save then," he jested.

Nancy grinned. "Is that all you think about, Byron? Saving others?"

He hesitated. In truth, it was what his life had become since the loss of his father—but now he had gained a wife. Well, almost. And in her presence, so many things that had mattered so much at the time seemed to fade away.

"You saved me," Byron said simply. "I'd like to help others."

Nancy lifted a hand and cupped his cheek, and such tenderness rushed through Byron, he thought for a moment he would melt into the mattress.

How was it possible that he had found such joy? How did he deserve such a woman?

"Well, now that we've saved almost everyone else," Nancy whispered, "can we concentrate on our happily-ever-after?"

Byron grinned. "I thought you'd never ask."

Their kiss was slow, passionate, and contained so much he could not say. And he knew, in that moment, that the rest of his life was only just beginning. This was the real adventure.

EPILOGUE

September 21, 1810

"**Y**OU AREN'T GOING to wear your hair like that, are you?"

Nancy smiled despite herself. "And what precisely is wrong with this?"

She tilted her head back and forth, examining herself in the large looking glass. The maid had been helpful, aiding her in pinning back her red curls, and she had thought the overall effect to be rather impressive.

That was not, however, the impression she had given. Apparently.

Beth's face appeared in the looking glass. "I mean, it's just like you always have your hair!"

Nancy nodded. "Precisely."

"But Nancy—"

"This is how I look," Nancy said firmly, picking up another pin and carefully ramming it into her hair to ensure that final curl would stay put. "I want to look how I look."

"But it's your wedding day!"

It was. Nancy could hardly believe it. After waiting for what felt like forever, it was strange to think it was today. Finally, after the long two weeks that she and Byron had been forced to wait for the banns to be read, they were getting married.

Within an hour.

"Well, I want Byron to be absolutely sure he is marrying the right woman," said Nancy aloud with a laugh. "And so I want to look like me."

"But—"

"Me, Beth," Nancy said, turning in her seat and looking at her sister. How could she make her understand? "Because it was me, me he fell in love with. Just a woman, not a duchess, or a countess, or a lady. Not someone with any money or any sway in the *ton*, or impressive looks, or anything like that."

Beth sat slowly onto the edge of her bed and nodded. "I see."

"I hope you do, because things are going to change," said Nancy, unable to help herself. "I thought—if I ever wed, that was—that things would stay the same."

But they wouldn't. This was a whole different life she was about to enter. Flutters of nerves rose across her chest. On one hand, she and Byron would return after today to the home they had already started making, to habits and routines they had already started to fall into.

Yet on the other hand, everything would be different.

She would be a duchess. The Duchess of Sedley. She would have to entertain, host, delight. She would enter society in a way she could never have imagined.

"The whole of London will be watching me," Nancy said quietly, hoping she could make her sister see. "Waiting for me to make a mistake, to not be the duchess they expect."

"But—"

"And that is why today, of all days, I have to be most myself," continued Nancy doggedly, trying not to think about the myriad of people she would be standing before in just a few short minutes. "I want them to see the woman Byron fell in love with; I want to be that woman. Just Nancy Mead. Just me."

The smile on her sister's face was warm. "I understand. Here, let me do that for you."

Nancy swallowed as she turned back to the looking glass and watched as her baby sister picked up their mother's string of pearls. Very carefully, Beth rested them around her neck and fiddled with the clasp.

Despite herself, Nancy raised a hand to touch them. The only connection they had to their mother, the only item of value they had not sold. And she would be wearing them today as she left behind the name of Mead and became a Renwick. A Sedley. The duchess.

"I wish Matthew was here," came her sister's soft words.

Nancy fought back tears. She was not going to cry on her wedding day, she told herself fiercely. Probably.

"He'll be sorry to miss out on the celebrations," she said aloud with as jocular a tone as she could manage.

As Nancy caught her sister's eye through the looking glass, she saw immediately Beth was not misled.

"You could always put off the wedding," Beth said. "Wait until I have had the chance to—"

"No, absolutely not," said Nancy firmly. The very idea of putting off the wedding...what would the *ton* think? Oh, she would never hear the end of it, the scandal!

It may even be bad enough, she thought, for Lady Romeril to renew her acquaintance with the family, if only to criticize her!

"No, I suppose not," said Beth, sitting beside her. "Not with all those late night excursions you have been making to Byron's bedchamber!"

Nancy's cheeks flushed red hot. Oh, it was awful to think anyone knew of that particular habit she and Byron had slipped into, but her baby sister? Quite enough to distract her, even if only momentarily, from thoughts of their brother.

"You are absolutely to forget that happened," she said, face burning.

Beth grinned. "You are a dark horse, Nancy! I never would have thought you—"

"I don't want to talk about it!" Nancy interrupted, rising from the seat by the looking glass and stepping around her bedchamber.

It was a pleasant room with an impressive aspect. The furniture was elegantly set out and the bed most comfortable. Not that she had spent much time sleeping in it, of course. But still. The few hours she had spent in it had been most acceptable.

But after today, after the events of a few hours' time, it would no longer be hers.

That was, it would not only be hers. The whole place would be hers, Byron had said just the other day.

"Not actually mine, though," Nancy had pointed out. "Not legally."

"It will be your home and that is all that matters," Byron had stated. "Your home. Our home."

Our home. Nancy swallowed, hardly able to believe this was happening. Just a month ago, she had never heard of the Duke of Sedley. All her thoughts had been on when they would receive Matthew's next letter. And now...

"I will attend the wedding, of course."

Nancy looked over at her sister, now seated by the looking glass. "I should think so!"

"And tomorrow I will—"

"Beth Mead, how many times have I told you, I absolutely forbid you from going to France!" Nancy said with a heavy sigh. "One would think you aren't listening to me!"

It was a conversation they'd had over and over again. Though Nancy could quite understand the impetus to travel to France, to search for Matthew who was surely wounded, she would not risk one sibling to rescue another.

"I will send someone," she said aloud, seeing the beginnings of an argument on her sister's brow. "Someone, but not you."

"But—"

"I am not jesting, Beth," Nancy stepped across the room and perched on the end of the bed with a stern expression. "Hear me?"

She had to be firm; this would be the last real effort she would make now to care for her sister. Because Byron had been right. Right in letting his brother go. There came a point, even if she had not known it before, when one had to allow siblings to make their own mistakes. Fight their own battles. Come up triumphant on their own.

Even if it hurt.

Wars, of course, did not count.

Beth glared. "I don't want to fight."

"Neither do—"

"Especially on your w-wedding day," said her sister with a sniff, and Nancy was astonished to see she was crying. "Mama would be so proud, and Papa would have w-wanted to walk you down the aisle."

Nancy's jaw tightened as every breath suddenly became difficult. Her sister was right.

"All the more reason to keep yourself safe," she said softly. "So Matthew and I can attend your wedding."

Beth rolled her eyes. "You think I'm going to have time to find a husband while I spend all this time looking after our brother?"

For an instant, just an instant, it was like looking into a mirror through time. Nancy's heart skipped a beat. Was that what she had been like? Always putting off life, never accepting she could have her own desires, her own wants and needs?

"Beth," Nancy said aloud, forcing those thoughts away. "I want you to promise you won't go to France without so much as a word!"

Her sister met her eye. "You want me to promise?"

"You must promise, or else I will not be leaving this room and poor old Byron will be left at the altar," said Nancy, trying to inject a little humor into her words as her heart thudded painfully. "Promise me, Beth."

Beth hesitated. "I...I will never feel at ease, you know. Until we find him."

EMILY E K MURDOCH

It was all Nancy could do not to agree with her. The trouble was, she had already been on an adventure to find a sibling. Though it was exciting, it was nothing compared to the danger she had been in—that they both had been in.

Today was supposed to be about celebration, and joy, and love.

"Promise me, Beth."

Her sister swallowed. "I promise."

Nancy's shoulders sagged. *Well, that was one challenge overcome today.* Just one more...

"We're going to be late, you know," Beth said conversationally.

"No, surely not," Nancy began, turning to the clock on the mantelpiece. "We—"

She froze. The hands pointed at ten to eleven. The wedding was at eleven o'clock.

Not the wedding. *Her wedding.*

"We're going to be late!" Nancy cried, dashing to the door as her sister giggled.

Late! Late to her own wedding! She would never hear the end of it. She had so much work to do, impressing the *ton*, and if she did not even arrive at the church in time—

"Nancy, wait!"

But she did not heed Beth's shouts as she rushed down the corridor toward the staircase. She had ten minutes—that would be sufficient time to get along the street and—

"Nancy!"

It was not her sister who cried out this time, but Byron. He was standing at the bottom of the staircase, eyes wide, as Nancy hurtled to a stop at the top.

"Shut your eyes!" cried her sister, panting as she pulled up beside her. "Byron, you're not supposed to see your bride before you meet at the altar!"

Nancy could not help but laugh as Byron immediately snapped his eyes shut, cheeks pinking.

"I didn't mean to—"

"This is why I said to wait!" Beth said severely, wagging a finger at Nancy. "So I could ensure this sort of disaster did not happen!"

But there was no malice in her sister's words, and all the tension which had grown between them in her bedchamber melted away. Nancy could not stop giggling as she came down the staircase, looking at Byron standing there, frozen with his eyes shut.

How did she deserve such happiness?

"Honestly, I would have thought the two of you would have organized around this," tutted Beth, following her down the stairs. "Really!"

"Go on outside, Beth, and walk along to the church and wait there for me," said Nancy, heart skipping a beat as she looked at Byron. "I need to talk to my future husband."

For the shortest of moments, Nancy thought her sister was going to argue with her. Then Beth nodded, brushed a quick kiss on her cheek, and stepped across the hall. The front door opened and closed.

"Is she gone?" asked Byron. "Can I open my eyes now?"

"Absolutely not!" Nancy said with a grin. "I can't have you seeing me in my wedding gown before you vow to marry me!"

"I cannot think you could be wearing anything," he said quietly, "that could make me change my mind."

Nancy's heart skipped a beat. He was such a good man. Would she have ever discovered that, unpeeled the layers of pain and passion that was Byron, if she had known he was a duke?

Almost certainly not. She would have been embarrassed, flushed at the mere thought of talking to a duke. He would have moved on to speak to another lady at a ball, or dinner, or card party, or wherever else they could have met. And that would have been it.

But now…

"You know, I am really happy to be marrying you," Nancy

said, stepping closer to the man she adored. He still had his eyes shut. "I love you, Byron."

"You have no idea how long I waited for you," he said softly. "Years. But this was the right time."

Brimming with happiness, Nancy leaned forward and kissed him. Byron responded immediately, pulling her into his arms and trailing kisses down her neck as her breath caught in her throat.

"Byron," she moaned. "We should—"

"Be quiet while I'm kissing you," he growled, though there was a teasing look on his brow.

Nancy slipped from his embrace but kept a hold of his hand. "Well, in that case, does that mean I shouldn't tell you what we're late for?"

Byron opened his eyes. "What are we—oh, Nancy…"

His voice trailed away.

Nancy flushed. She had meant what she had said to her sister upstairs in her bedchamber. She really did want to look like herself on her wedding day.

But that didn't mean she couldn't look like the absolute best version of herself.

And that was why, despite her maid's raised eyebrows, she had refused Byron's offer to have a special gown made at the most impressive modiste in London. She already had a gown that spoke of Byron's generosity, and his impulsiveness, and the way she felt when he looked at her.

"But…but isn't that—"

"This is the gown you bought me while on the road," Nancy confirmed with a smile, brushing her fingers across the floral patterned silk. "The gown you bought me after you'd kissed me rotten—"

"You didn't know I was a duke then," Byron said with a wry smile. "Goodness. You look—you look wonderful."

"But we're still late," Nancy pointed out.

"For church? Oh, you have much to learn about being a duchess, Nancy," he said as they stepped forward together to the wide double doors that opened out to the carriage awaiting them. "And I can't wait to teach you."

Nancy's heart overflowed with happiness. "Well, we have the rest of our lives. All the time in the world."

About Emily E K Murdoch

If you love falling in love, then you've come to the right place.

I am a historian and writer and have a varied career to date: from examining medieval manuscripts to designing museum exhibitions, to working as a researcher for the BBC to working for the National Trust.

My books range from England 1050 to Texas 1848, and I can't wait for you to fall in love with my heroes and heroines!

Follow me on twitter and instagram @emilyekmurdoch, find me on facebook at facebook.com/theemilyekmurdoch, and read my blog at www.emilyekmurdoch.com.

CPSIA information can be obtained
at www.ICGtesting.com
Printed in the USA
BVHW050010160623
666010BV00013B/1226